MOTHER KNOWS MESS!

MOTHER KNOWS MESS!

JAMES M. PEGUES

XULON PRESS

Xulon Press
555 Winderley Pl, Suite 225
Maitland, FL 32751
407.339.4217
www.xulonpress.com

© 2024 by James M. Pegues

All rights reserved solely by the author. The author guarantees all contents are original and do not infringe upon the legal rights of any other person or work. No part of this book may be reproduced in any form without the permission of the author.

Due to the changing nature of the Internet, if there are any web addresses, links, or URLs included in this manuscript, these may have been altered and may no longer be accessible. The views and opinions shared in this book belong solely to the author and do not necessarily reflect those of the publisher. The publisher therefore disclaims responsibility for the views or opinions expressed within the work.

Paperback ISBN-13: 978-1-66289-854-9
Ebook ISBN-13: 978-1-66289-855-6

Table of Contents

Chapter 1	Mother's confrontation with the Aintwright's	1
Chapter 2	Pastor and First Lady stopped by Mother's house	21
Chapter 3	Mothers three favorite girls stopped by to gossip	29
Chapter 4	Mother's lies causes trouble between the church members	35
Chapter 5	Mother's lies brought everyone to their boiling point	47
Chapter 6	Missionary Scareaway is engaged to be married	63
Chapter 7	Toddie and the Scareaway's have a face off	73
Chapter 8	The Liketalies went up against Mother Rongway	85
Chapter 9	Toddie's encounter with the Backnibblers	93
Chapter 10	Things began to heat up at Mother's house	99
Chapter 11	Minister Wannado shocks Toddie and Mother	109
Chapter 12	A wedding rehearsal unlike any other	117
Chapter 13	Minister Wannado showed off his preaching skills	129
Chapter 14	Mother Rongway went too far	137

CHAPTER 1

MOTHER'S CONFRONTATION WITH THE AINTWRIGHTS

It was early morning in a little, old town in South Carolina appropriately named Rongway Peaks. It was a typical small town, closed in by some beautiful mountains on one side and a lush green valley on the other side. It was a quiet town where nothing exciting ever happened. It had one main street with one stop light. There was only one sheriff because there was not any crime. The sheriff had, on a few occasions, given out a jaywalking ticket. No one ever got a speeding ticket because no one was ever in a hurry to get anywhere. Everyone here knew everyone else by name. It was a neighborly town where you did not even have to lock your door at night. By all accounts, this was a perfect little Southern town and a wonderful place to live. But as the saying goes, you cannot judge a book by its cover.

A woman lived there by the name of Rosalee Rongway, or better known as Mother Rongway. The Rongways had a long history in this town. Mother Rongway's great-great-grandfather, Leroy Rongway, was one of the town founders. That was where the name Rongway Peaks came from. Her great-grandfather, Bishop Jonathan Rongway, founded the Rongway First Liberation Church and pastored it for many years before he died. After that, her grandfather, Thomas Rongway, took the church over and pastored it for many years before he died. Then, for the last ten years, her father, William Rongway, pastored the church. It was the only church for miles around, so everyone religious went there.

A week had passed since Mother Rongway's father died, and they had held the funeral just the day before. Mother Rongway got up early that morning and was sitting at the kitchen table drinking coffee. At that moment her husband, Deacon John Rongway, came into the kitchen. He told Mother Rongway, "You are looking peachy keen this morning," trying to be a loving husband. But Mother Rongway, being true to who she was, gave him a dirty look and said to him, "You still look like a frog to me." Deacon Rongway poured himself a cup of coffee and sat at the table with his wife. He began to tell her, "I was just trying to comfort you, seeing that your father died only a week ago, and please do not start fussing."

Now, I know what you are thinking. No, Mother Rongway did not marry her brother. Mother Rongway was an only child, so when she got married, her husband had to agree to take the Rongway name. Her father did not have a boy to continue his name, and he wanted to make sure the Rongway name lived on. Since Mother Rongway was an only child, she inherited the church. She was raised in the church and watched her father do a lot of questionable things. Her Mother sat back and neither did nor said anything about the late Pastor Rongway's behavior. Her father got several young women in his church pregnant. He was accused of molesting little boys, but there was not enough proof to convict him. Many people were afraid of him, so no one came forth to accuse him. Mother Rongway had issues since her childhood. Now we all know that a zebra cannot change its stripes, and Mother Rongway could not change who she was. Everything had to be her way. She used everything she heard about her friends to her advantage.

She began to tell John, "You never tried to comfort me while my father was alive, so I do not need you trying to comfort me now." So, John, still trying to be a loving, caring husband, asked her, "Why are you acting like this? Your father was a good man, and he left you the church, which you know is a gold mine." Mother Rongway looked at him with a frown on her face and hesitated a moment before she spoke. Then she said to him, "I know my father was not a good man, and he treated you like dirt no matter how much you sucked up. I know my church is a gold mine, and you are not going to get your grimy little hands on any of it." Deacon Rongway realized he could not win talking to Mother Rongway, so he finished his coffee and got up to leave. But before he went out, he said something that he should not have said. He told her, "You win, and I should disappear for a little while so you can get yourself together." Mother Rongway chuckled, looked at him over her glasses, and said to him with a strong voice, "You should be careful what you say. People disappear all the time. You might end up disappearing permanently." Deacon Rongway replied, "Whatever," then left.

Deacon John Rongway's last name was Wilson before he was told he was marrying Mother Rongway. He was born and raised in Rongway Peaks. He never knew who his father was, and his mother died when he was in his early twenties. He had an older brother who moved away when their mother died, and the two of them had not spoken or seen one another since. Everyone in Rongway Peaks knew deacon Rongway and liked him. He was always quiet and kept to himself and was a faithful member of the church. He was all alone, which made him a prime candidate to marry Mother Rongway, and her father did not give him another choice. Mother Rongway finished her coffee and went grocery shopping.

Another week passed, and it was another beautiful morning in Rongway Peaks. Mother got up early and began to straighten up the living room. She turned on her special music that she listened to only when no one else was around and began to dance. Because she was old school, the only dances she knew were the twist, the running man, the robot and, well, you get the picture. Just when she really got into her groove, the doorbell rang. She scrambled to play some gospel music and put on her church face. She composed herself as she went to the door. Then she shouted with a loving voice to ask who was at the door. A voice from outside the door shouted back and said, "It's me, Deacon

Aintwright. Can I come in?" Mother opened the door, greeting him and saying, "Come on in and sit awhile." She walked over and turned the music off, and they both sat down. Then the deacon said, "I was just in the area and thought I would stop by to talk if you have the time." Mother smiled and let him know that she always had time for him and would always be available for him.

Now you may notice that Mother was talking in her sweet, loving voice, but do not get sucked in! She could flip the script on you in a minute. Then Deacon Aintwright got brave and began to question Mother. He said to her, "When I rang the doorbell, I thought I heard some worldly music playing." Mother reassured him he had not heard any worldly music in her house. She said, "My house is a God-fearing house, and I do not allow that kind of music in my house." Deacon Aintwright insisted that he had heard worldly music, telling her that his ears did not fool him. He said to her, "I would know that music anywhere." Why did he go there? Mother's voice changed just that quick from sweet and loving to mean and harsh. Mother stood up, and with her hands on her hips and her head moving from side to side, she let Deacon Aintwright have it. In one of the scariest voices the deacon had ever heard Mother Rongway use (he could have sworn her head spun around), she screamed, asking him, "Who you going to believe? Me or your lying ears? When I say you did not hear any worldly music in my house, you did not hear any worldly music, and that is all there is to it!" Shaking and trying to compose himself, Deacon Aintwright quickly remembered who he was talking to and changed the conversation. He told Mother with a weak, trembling voice, "It is all right with me; whatever you say. Please calm down, because I was not accusing you of anything. I just stopped by to get some motherly advice.

Mother Rongway took a deep breath and slowly composed herself. She sat back down and remembered that Deacon Aintwright said he wanted to talk to her about something, so she told him to start talking. At that point Deacon Aintwright broke down almost to tears. He still had not completely recovered from Mother's tongue-lashing and felt emotional about what he wanted to talk to her about. With a trembling, squeaky voice, he told Mother, "I just got fired from my job." Mother could not believe what she was hearing. Looking at him with disgust, she asked him, "What did you do to get fired?" Deacon Aintwright began to explain. He said, "I told them people at my job that I needed more than an hour for lunch, but they would not listen." Mother Rongway shook her head in disbelief. In her mind she was thinking, *This man is saying that an hour is not enough time for him to eat lunch, but he must be joking.* She asked him, "Do you need two hours for lunch?" Then she thought to herself, *How much does he eat? He must be playing a joke on me.* The deacon began to say, "I am a slow eater, and sometimes I like to take a little nap after I eat." Mother Rongway still could not believe what she was hearing and asked the deacon, "Are you kidding me?" He told her that he was not kidding and said, "I kept telling them people I worked for that they wanted me to be at work too early in the morning. I was late a few times, but I never missed a day. I gave them people ten years and could have had a career at that job." Now Mother was curious, so she asked him, "What time did you have to be at work every morning?" Deacon Aintwright must have had some issues, because his answer did not sound like that of someone who was normal. He told Mother, "I had to be to work at eleven o'clock each morning, but I need my sleep."

Now Mother was almost in shock listening to what the deacon was saying. She shook her head in disbelief as she tried to reason this thing out. She said to him, "You need more than an hour for lunch, and you could not be to work by eleven o'clock? I would have fired you too. Where did you work?" Now, you would think because of the way he was acting that he must have been working at some Fortune 500 company, but that was not the case. He looked at Mother Rongway with a serious face and told her, "I worked at the Burger Shack." He stood up and strutted around with his chest out and told Mother, "I was the main cook, and the best they had, and they threw me out like an old hamburger." Then he sat back down. Mother Rongway looked at

Deacon Aintwright, thinking, *There must be something wrong with this brother, and now his story is getting hilarious.* Mother looked at him with a straight face and told him, "They are always hiring at Bigger Burger," and began to laugh uncontrollably. But Deacon Aintwright did not see anything funny. He told Mother, "I don't know how to break the news to my wife, because we had big dreams. And now that I don't have a job, I know she will be mad."

Now, a real church mother would have tried to console the deacon, but that was not who Mother Rongway was. She dropped a bomb on the deacon that he never saw coming. Mother stopped laughing, and her mood changed instantly. She looked at the deacon and told him, "You should be all right. Your wife works, and with the money you steal from the church offering every week, you should have enough money to do whatever you and your wife desire to do." Deacon Aintwright was stunned. He thought he was careful and was sure no one knew. It was such a small amount, he was sure no one would even notice that any money was missing.

You see, Deacon Aintwright had a slight problem. His friends knew him by the name Cletus. When he was a small child, his Mother would take him to the store and hide packs of meat in his clothes because they never had enough money for food. Finally, his mom got caught stealing and went to prison. His father left, and the deacon got stuck raising his little brother on the streets. Stealing was all he knew. It was the only way he knew how to survive. At age eighteen, he got caught stealing and was sentenced to five years in prison. Once he got out of prison, he went into a rehab program to get his life back on track. The rehab center was where he met his wife, who introduced him to church. Now, it appeared he may have backslid.

At this point, he got up and walked around nervously, trying to figure out how to respond. Then he tried to act like he did not know what Mother Rongway was talking about. "What money, and what are you talking about?" he asked with a tremble in his voice. Mother Rongway never missed a beat. She told him, "You must have forgotten who you are talking to. May I remind you that the church belongs to me, and I know everything that goes on there? I know stuff that Pastor Whocares does not know." Now Deacon Aintwright realized he was backed into a corner and must find a way out alive. The only thing he could think to do at that moment was to produce a lie, and then lie some more. So, he told Mother, "You got it all wrong. I was just making change for a twenty-dollar bill for someone and must have accidentally given them too much money back, that is all." Mother gave him a look that said, *"Do you think I am stupid?"* She said, "You must have given back too much change a whole lot of Sundays, because this has been going on for a while, and I have not said anything until now." The deacon realized that lying had not worked and had to find something else.

"We can ask Deacon Rongway, because he can vouch for me." Then he realized no one had seen Deacon Rongway all week, so he asked Mother Rongway where her husband was. Mother always had an answer, even if she must lie, so she told him, "Deacon Rongway went out of town to take care of his sick mother." But Deacon Aintwright quickly pointed out to her that she was lying. He said to her, "May I remind you that Deacon Rongway's mother died two years ago, and I attended the funeral." It was hard to back Mother Rongway into a corner. She always had another way out. She looked at Deacon Aintwright with a serious face and said to him, "There go them lying ears again. I said, 'sick brother' and you heard 'sick mother.'" Then she said, "Deacon Rongway will not ever turn up again," but she corrected herself and said, "I meant to say he may not come back until spring." Most people would think that what Mother had just said sounded very suspicious, but Deacon Aintwright was too busy trying to save himself, so he did not give it another thought.

Now, he got down to some serious begging. He said to Mother, "I will go along with whatever you say and not say anything to anybody if you will give me a chance to explain. You have judged me all wrong, because this is all a big misunderstanding." Mother Rongway always used every opportunity to her advantage. It did not matter who or what it was, she would find a way to come out on top. No one had ever been able to get the upper hand against her; many people had tried and found out the hard way. Deacon Aintwright did not know it yet but would soon learn that he had just given Mother Rongway the ammunition she needed to blackmail him. She went into her sweet, motherly act and pulled out her sweet, motherly voice again. She said to the deacon, "I'm not judging you, baby, and the fact that you have been stealing from the church offering can be our little secret." Now the deacon knew something was up, because this conversation had just gone in a whole different direction. So, he asked Mother Rongway, "What do you mean by 'This can be our little secret?' Just what do you have in mind?"

At this point Mother Rongway stood up and turned her back to Deacon Aintwright and walked away. She put on her sad face and sad voice and said something that shocked the deacon. She told him, "Since my husband died, oops—I meant to say, 'went away,' I get so lonely. Now that is where you come in. If you should just happen to be in the neighborhood and stop by my house at least once a month to ease my loneliness, your secret will never leave this house." At this point, Deacon Aintwright could not believe what he was hearing. Here this woman was, *the* mother of the church, a supposed Godly woman, saying this. He tried to compose himself, but now fear had really taken over. He stood there not knowing how to respond. Mother kept her back to him and with a stern voice said, "I'm waiting for an answer." Finally, Deacon Aintwright began to speak with a tremble in his voice, almost in tears. He said to her, "I know you cannot be saying what I think you are saying, and besides that, you are old and wrinkled. Even if I do what you are proposing, if my wife finds out, she will kill me." That did not bother Mother at all. She turned around and walked over to where the deacon stood and put her hand on his shoulder. She switched back to that sweet, loving, motherly voice and said, "The way I see it, you do not have any other choice, but you should pray about it." Deacon Aintwright moved her hand from his shoulder and began to walk around nervously while thinking to himself, *"What am I going to do?"* He knew he was in trouble and must find a way out somehow. Mother Rongway was not somebody you wanted to cross. She would use every opportunity to get what she wanted. Now the deacon was nervous, and it was like being in quicksand, the more he wiggled, the more he sank. So, he spoke out of desperation and shouted, "Pray about it! You have that sickness some people get when they get old, all-hammers, or something like that. You must have lost your mind." Mother Rongway looked at Deacon Aintwright and, with a little chuckle in her voice, told him, "You lost your mind when you started stealing from my church. You must have that sickness a lot of people get at any age, all-crook, or something like that."

Suddenly, Deacon Aintwright had a revelation. He believed he had a way out of this whole situation. He let Mother know that he was not going to fall for her little extortion scheme. He informed her, "I'm going to go and confess everything to Pastor Whocares and do whatever Pastor tells me to do." At that moment, Deacon Aintwright began feeling much better because he believed he had found a way out, but Mother Rongway burst his bubble in a hurry. Mother began to laugh like she had really lost her mind, which now really confused the deacon. He asked Mother, "What are you laughing about? Because I do not see anything funny. Maybe if you let me in on the joke, I can laugh too." Mother managed to compose herself a little but kept laughing. Then she told the deacon something that took all the wind out of his sails. She asked him, "Are you talking about Pastor Whocares, pastor of the Rongway First Liberation Church?" He said, "Yes, I am." Mother said, "I tell pastor Whocares what to do."

Poor Deacon Aintwright now had no supporting arguments. He was in a tricky situation and did not know what to do. He told Mother, "All this time I was just thinking you was crazy, but now I know for sure you are crazy." He was thinking that this could not be happening, this must be a bad dream or something, but Mother Rongway just kept applying the pressure. She kept talking in her loving, motherly voice and said something that completely blew Deacon Aintwright away. She asked him, "How do you think the church got its name? My family founded the church, and it was passed down to me. I put Pastor Whocares up as pastor, and if he does not do what I tell him to do, I will take him down and find myself another pastor who will." Deacon Aintwright was trying to keep it together, but at that point he knew he was finished. He sat down, grabbed his head, looked up toward heaven and began to say, "Out of all the towns in this world, and all the churches in this world, how did I end up in this town at this church?" Mother Rongway, still talking in her sweet voice, told him, "If you try to leave my church, I will have no other choice but to have you thrown in jail for stealing."

Now Deacon Aintwright was really upset. He jumped up out of his seat and got loud. He asked her, "What kind of church mother are you? I came to you for some motherly advice, and you turned out to be Lucifer's mother." Mother put both hands on her hips and began moving her head side to side again. Now talking in her other voice, she let the deacon have it again with both barrels. She called him Deacon Kleptomaniac and said, "If I'm the devil's mother, you must be the devil's nephew. Anyway, all you have to do is what I tell you to do, and there will not be a problem at all." But as you can imagine, the deacon did not see it that way. Still terribly upset, he very loudly told her, "You are blackmailing me to cheat on my wife and threatening to have me put in jail if I do not! There is a problem!" Mother Rongway switched back to her sweet, loving voice and even called him *sweetheart*. She spoke softly and said, "I see it as a blessing for you. The Lord always gives us choices, and you have a choice," and she ended her statement by calling him *baby*.

Mother had to have more than one personality. One minute she was this sweet, loving, motherly person, then the next minute she was like the devil's spawn. The deacon did not stand a chance. If he did what she said, he would be in trouble, and if he did not do what she said, he would be in trouble. Still trying to defend himself, he told Mother Rongway, "Leave the Lord out of this conversation." He told her this was all her doing. By now you know that Mother Rongway would not be outdone. She said to him, "The way I see it, we are two of a kind. People do say that birds of a feather flock together." Deacon Aintwright did not feel that at all. He told her, "That may be what people say, but I'm an eagle, and I'm going to find a way to fly out of your mess." Mother Rongway began to laugh again. Then she said to him, "You must have meant *turkey*, and I have news for you—turkeys do not fly." She told him he was in this "mess," as he called it, until she decided—*if* she decided—to let him out. He said to her, "I'm sure we can work out a deal."

Suddenly a light came on in his head. He had another revelation and knew how he could get out of Mother's grip. He told her he knew exactly what he could do, as he strutted around again like he had just hit the jackpot. He told her, "I will get two jobs and pay the church back the money I borrowed, and everything will be all right." So now he was feeling good about himself again and had a big smile on his face, because he had a way out—so he thought. Mother Rongway soon burst his balloon again and wiped that smile off his face. Mother started laughing again and told him, "You can't even keep one job, so I know you could not keep two, so you've got to come up with something better than that."

He now had to try and produce something better than that. So, he sat down and realized he was right back where he was in the beginning of all this. He dropped his head down in despair and told Mother, "I do not know what else I can do, because I am not about to have an affair with you. I would rather go to jail first." But his despair did not bother Mother Rongway at all. She told him not to think of it as an affair but to think of it as his reasonable service. She went on to say, "The Bible said to take care of the widows." Wait a minute, did she just say *widow*? So, Deacon Aintwright's curiosity replaced his fear for a minute, and he began to question Mother again. He asked her, "Where did you say

Deacon Rongway is?" But Mother, being quick on her feet, replied, "I did not mean to say *widows*; I meant to say, take care of the *mothers*."

The deacon was getting suspicious and a little fearful. Something was not right, but he was afraid to ask any more questions about Deacon Rongway, so he left that subject alone. He told Mother, "I thought you was just a wrinkled, dried-up old prune, but you are a long way past that. You do not have all-hammers, but you have mental problems; you must be crazy." Mother Rongway did not waste any time but fired right back at him, "I may have mental problems but right now, you have bigger problems than I have. You stole money from my church, and one way or another, you are going to pay." So, the deacon stood back up and began to pace around the room, almost at the point of panicking. He was like a rat that had been caught in a trap, trying everything to escape with seemingly no way out. Now he knew, without any doubt, that he could not outsmart, outtalk, or outthink Mother Rongway. So, as they say, he admitted defeat. He told her that right then she seemed to be holding all the cards. Then he said, "What goes around comes around, and one day you are going to get paid back for all the dirty tricks and games you use against people."

Now there was defeat in Deacon Aintwright's voice. All the fight that he thought he had in him was gone. He was like a poor little puppy, cowering in a corner with his tail between his legs. Mother Rongway thrived on the fear of others. The deacon was now like clay in her hands, and she had him right where she wanted him. She walked over to where sat and placed her hand on his shoulder again. Then, using her sweet, loving, motherly voice, she asked him, "Whatever do you mean? I am Mother Rongway, and I always get my way. Your little idle threats do not scare me, so you might as well stop wasting your breath." At this point, Deacon Aintwright did not know what he should do. Frustrated to the point of almost *really* having a panic attack, he got up and headed toward the door, telling Mother Rongway, "I have to get out of your house. It was a mistake coming here in the first place, and I should not have stopped by. I do not know what I was thinking."

Just before Deacon Aintwright got to the door, the doorbell rang, so he stopped. Mother went to the door, and to her and Deacon Aintwright's surprise, it was Sister Aintwright. Mother Rongway put on her best sweet, loving voice, as if everything were all right. She spoke and gave Sister Aintwright a big hug and told her to come on in. Then Mother asked her, "What brings you by today, baby?" Sister Aintwright was in an exceptionally good mood. It was a beautiful day, and she was out just enjoying life. She had no clue what she had walked into. She told Mother Rongway, "I was out doing a little shopping, and I saw my husband's car in your driveway and decided to stop and see what he is doing here." She spoke to her husband and walked over and gave him a kiss. To say the least, Deacon Aintwright was nervous as he spoke. He told her, "I was not expecting to see you at Mother Rongway's house today." With a chuckle in her voice, she told him, "I bet you wasn't, but you never know where I might turn up, so you better be walking a straight line all the time."

Now Mother Rongway saw another chance to throw some more wood on the fire. Once again using her best motherly voice, she told the two of them to sit down and relax so they could talk for a while. They all sat down. She began to tell Sister Aintwright, "Before you got here, the deacon and I was having a wonderful conversation." Then she asked the deacon to agree. Now, as you can imagine, this put Deacon Aintwright in a tight spot. He tried to speak in his normal voice, so his wife would not know something was wrong. He put a phony grin on his face and reluctantly spoke. He said, "Yes, it was just so wonderful and revealing. I did not know Mother Rongway was so full of knowledge." So naturally Sister Aintwright asked what the two of them had been talking about that was so wonderful. She said, "I would love to hear it." Just what Mother Rongway wanted to hear. Mother Rongway never missed an opportunity to put someone on the spot. She saw another chance to make Deacon Aintwright squirm. She told the deacon, "You should tell Sister Aintwright what we were talking about because I know she will love hearing it coming from you." What can you do when you know you are guilty? What can you say?

Deacon Aintwright began to speak slowly, trying to figure out what he should say, so he quickly made up a lie. He told sister Aintwright, "Mother and I were talking about the goodness of the Lord and how He is a blessing at the church." Sister Aintwright, now excited, said, "I know that is right. The way you and Mother Rongway were dancing all over the church last Sunday made me want to cut a step, and you both know I do not have a dance." So, at that moment, Mother Rongway stood up and told them, "You two lovebirds have to excuse me for a minute or two. I need to go to the little girls' room." Sister Aintwright said to Mother Rongway, "Me and Cletus do not have anywhere to be, so you can take your time." Mother left the room, and the deacon saw his chance to get out of that house. He waited until Mother Rongway got completely out of the room, jumped up, and began to plead with his wife to leave Mother's house before she came back into the room. He looked around and walked over near the door that Mother had gone out of to make sure that she could not hear him, and told his wife, "We got to leave; we got to get out of this crazy woman's house." Now Bertha Mae, Sister Aintwright's first name, was confused. So, she asked Cletus, "What are you talking about, and what crazy woman are you talking about?"

He was still standing near the door that Mother left through to be sure she was not coming back yet. Then he told his wife, "Mother Rongway is the crazy woman. She has lost all her marbles, she is out to lunch, she is not playing with a full deck of cards, her elevator does not go all the way up—however you want to say it. That woman is crazy." Sister Aintwright looked at him with confusion. Then she told him, "Something must be wrong with you, because Mother Rongway is one of the sweetest mothers we know." He agreed that was what he had thought too but went on to say, "Mother is like Jekyll and Hyde, and she got everybody believing she is this nice, loving, caring mother, but now I know better." Sister Aintwright got up and walked over to

Mother's Confrontation with the Aintwrights

where the deacon was standing and put her hand on his head to see if he had a fever, because to her, he was talking crazy. At this point Deacon Aintwright got really upset and asked her, "Why won't you believe me?"

Then he reluctantly began to confess. He told her, "Mother found out that I have been borrowing a little money from the church offering, and she told me if I do not have an affair with her, she will have me put in jail." Sister Aintwright began to laugh uncontrollably as she replied, "Do you expect me to believe that Mother Rongway, that sweet, little, old woman, propositioned you, out of all the men in the church? I do not mean any harm, but you are not all that." Deacon Aintwright stopped her before she could say anything else. He agreed, then said, "I may not be the most desirable man at the church, but we need to get out of this house, even out of this town." Sister Aintwright sat down, shaking her head, still not sure if she believed what Cletus was saying. She said to him, "If I am to believe your story about Mother Rongway, then I must believe that you are stealing from the church again. We had to leave the last church because you got caught stealing, and here you go again." But the deacon insisted it was not true and said, "At the last church, that was all a big misunderstanding, and they never proved anything, anyway."

Now sister Aintwright was getting upset and told him, "I will not go to jail because of you. I will get a divorcement fir fiffst." He tried to calm her down by telling her that nobody was going to jail. He said, "Mother Rongway is a reasonable woman, and I am sure we can work something out. By the way, what is a divorcement? I think you meant divorce. We do not need a divorce." Now sister Aintwright was really upset. She told him, "I do not care anymore, and the Bible says to stay married until theft do us part." The deacon looked at her a little confused and said, "I do not know much about the Bible, but I am quite sure it says until death do us part, not theft do us part." At that point, Bertha Mae said, "I am done, I've had it, and you need some professional help." The deacon disagreed and said, "I do not need any professional help, because I have learned my lesson this time." At this point, sister Aintwright started talking very loudly. She told him, "That is what you said the last time, and we are right back here again, and you are not even a good crook, because you get caught every time." He tried to calm her down and told her, "You need to lower your voice so Mother Rongway does not hear you! I get the point." Sister Aintwright, still trying to understand, asked him, "What were you thinking, and why did you stop by Mother's house in the first place?" Once again, reluctantly, Deacon Aintwright began to come clean. He told her, "I got fired from my job today and was feeling bad and stopped by to talk to Mother. I was thinking she could give me some good motherly advice." Still upset, Sister Aintwright told him, "I am glad you got fired, and maybe now you will get a real job like a real man."

Deacon Aintwright still stood near the door where Mother had gone out so he could hear her when she decided to come back, and now he walked over to where his wife was sitting and told her, "I will agree with anything you say, but we need to get out of here before Mother Rongway comes back in the room." But Sister Aintwright, now thinking a little clearer, told him, "We cannot leave like we are sneaking out; that would be so rude. I think I need to have a word or two with Mother." Now the deacon got nervous again. He told Bertha Mae, "You do not need to make a spectacle out of yourself. We should just go and leave well enough alone." Sister Aintwright was raised in Africa. Her father worked as a law enforcer, and her mother did not work. Things were okay in Africa where her family lived, but poverty reached the masses. One day there was an outpouring of violence, and she and her mother had to escape to America. The transition from Africa to America had been very scary, but they made it. She saw a lot of death along the journey, and only she and her mother had made it. They never heard from nor saw her father again. A few years after being in America, her mother died. She had to grow up and be strong. She went to college and graduated with a psychology degree.

She began to work for a rehab center, where she became a program director. She met her husband at the center. Her life taught her not to back down from a fight, but she had never come up against anybody like Mother Rongway.

She told Cletus, "Do not worry about anything, because I got this. I will be cool and calm, but I need to have a few words with Mother to clear the air." The deacon said to her, "That is the problem—I know you; we need to get out of here right now." At that moment, Mother Rongway came back into the room not knowing what the Aintwrights had been discussing. She apologized that it took her so long but explained and said, "I was on the phone with Mother Runnamouth, and I thought she would never hang up." Sister Aintwright told Mother Rongway, "That is all right, because me and Cletus were just sitting here talking and laughing, waiting for you to come back." Mother said that was good, then chuckled and said, "I hope you two were not talking about me." Sister Aintwright, trying to stay cool and calm, said to Mother, "There are a few things I need to discuss with you, if you have time." Deacon Aintwright, now a nervous wreck, pled with Bertha Mae to just leave things alone. Mother Rongway immediately went into her sweet, motherly role. She spoke with such a loving voice and asked the question, "Leave what alone? What do you want to talk to me about?"

At that point, Sister Aintwright lost it, jumping up and getting loud. Deacon Aintwright grabbed her and tried to hold her back. Shouting at the top of her voice, she asked Mother, "Where do you get off propositioning my husband? What would make you think he would want some old, wrinkled-up grandmother like you?" Mother Rongway, still talking in a calm, sweet voice, told Sister Aintwright, "You need to calm down, sweetheart. You look like you are about to have a stroke." Sister Aintwright said to Mother, "I am about to have a stroke all right; I'm about to stroke my fist upside your old head." Deacon Aintwright was still trying to keep Sister Aintwright from getting to Mother. He started shouting at her as he tried to hold her back. He told her, "You need to calm down and leave it alone. It is not worth anybody getting hurt." At this point, Mother Rongway balled up her fist, ready to fight if she must. She told the deacon, "Do not hold Sister Aintwright back; let her go. I have not had a good workout in a long time." Sister Aintwright was furious, and she really began to shout at Mother Rongway. She told Mother, "How dare you? Being the mother of the church, acting like this. I will give you a workout, all right, but when I am finished, you will not need a sport drink; you will need life support."

Now you would think that this would have made Mother Rongway a little nervous, but you must remember who this was! Still using her sweet, motherly voice, she asked Sister Aintwright, "Do you really think I would let you hurt me? I did not get to be as old as I am by being stupid." Then she had the nerve to call Sister Aintwright "baby." Finally, Deacon Aintwright spoke up to defuse the situation. He told Mother Rongway, "You should go back into the room where you just came from, and we will leave and forget everything that happened." Now you would think leaving was a good idea. After all, if the Aintwrights left, the problem would be solved, right? But Sister Aintwright was not ready to let it go yet. She told Cletus, "You can leave if you want to, but I am not going anywhere. After what you told me, I think Mother needs to be taught a lesson, and I am the teacher." At this point, Mother Rongway walked over to the coffee table and picked up her handbag. She told sister Aintwright, "Do not make me laugh, because I will tell you what is going to happen. You are going to let your husband's lies get you shot. I like you and do not want to have to shoot you." Sister Aintwright was shocked and replied by saying, "What!" Then she shouted at Cletus to turn her loose. She told him, "This old woman is calling you a liar and threatening to shoot me. If you are not man enough to do something, I will."

When she said that, Deacon Aintwright turned her loose and got upset by her comment about his manhood. He told her, "This does not have anything to do with my manhood; it is only common sense.

We should just leave before somebody does something stupid. This is all a big misunderstanding, and I know that we all will be laughing about it later." Bertha Mae began to laugh and gesture up in Cletus's face, asking him, "Have you lost your ridiculous mind? I thought I married a man. Where is your backbone? I did not know I married a scared little boy. Do you need your mama to come here and fight for you?" This really got under Cletus's skin, and he tried to pull out his manhood. He told Bertha Mae, "That is enough. You need to back up off me. Do not get me mad, because I will not be responsible for what I might do." But Sister Aintwright kept pushing and asked him, "Are you a man or a mouse? Are you going to let this unholy woman disrespect me and talk to you like you are a nobody?" Mother Rongway saw another chance to turn up the heat and keep trouble going. Once again, she used her sweet, loving, motherly voice as she spoke. She told Sister Aintwright, "You must know you married a girly man. The deacon needs to go home, put on a dress, and do housework, because he sure is not a man." Now this really upset Deacon Aintwright, and he went off. He got loud and told Mother, "You need to wait one minute. I was trying to be nice and keep Bertha Mae from taking you apart, but I am about to come over there where you are and slap that broke-down wig right off your old head." But before he could do anything, Sister Aintwright caught him by his arm because she did not want him to get himself in trouble. She told him, "Hold up, hotshot. Don't do anything stupid. Should I remind you that you have a record from the past, and if you hit somebody, you will go to jail for certain? I will take care of Mother myself."

Mother Rongway had had enough of this back-and-forth, so she laid it on the line. She told them, "I think you both need to leave my house right now. I will shoot you both and tell everybody how the two of you came to my house and went crazy, and I had to shoot you to keep you from hurting me. You know everyone will believe me because I am Mother Rongway." Then she looked at them with a big smile on her face. Once again Sister Aintwright was surprised at what came out of Mother's mouth. She looked at her husband and told him, "You are right, and I now see for myself that Mother Rongway is crazy. We need to get out of this house, from around this drama mama, before I lose my religion." So, the deacon and Sister Aintwright hurried out the door as Mother Rongway shouted. She told her, "That was a joke, because you never had any religion." She told them both never to come back to her house again. Mother Rongway slammed the door and began straightening up the living room as she tried to calm down.

CHAPTER 2

Pastor and First Lady Stopped by Mother's House

A few minutes passed, and the doorbell rang. Mother went to the door hoping the Aintwrights had not returned. She put her guard back up and shouted with a loud, angry voice to ask who was at her door. A nice, calm voice shouted from outside the door and said, "Praise the Lord, Mother, it is the Pastor and First Lady Whocares." Mother quickly changed her voice and attitude as she opened the door. Then, with her loving, motherly voice, she said, "My pastor and first lady. Praise the Lord, what a pleasant surprise." She told them to come on in and that she was so glad to see them. First Lady Whocares replied and said to Mother, "You are acting like you have not seen us in months." Mother Rongway settled back into her motherly role. Using her sweet, motherly voice, she told the first lady, "No, that is not the case at all. I just love my pastor and first lady because you two are so special in my heart." Pastor Whocares asked Mother, "Was that Deacon and Sister Aintwright leaving when we drove up?" Mother told him, "It was, and me and the Aintwrights spent a few lovely hours together talking about the goodness of the Lord."

The pastor replied, "The way they sped out of here, I hope everything is all right at their house." The first lady agreed and said, "The way they flew out of the driveway, you would think they were going somewhere to fight a fire." But Mother Rongway always had an answer. She told them, "There was not anything wrong. They were probably racing each other. Everybody knows how those two lovebirds like to play sometimes." Pastor Whocares agreed with Mother and added, "Those two do act like a couple of teenagers at times." The first lady had a different view on how their behavior was. She said, "They act weird if you ask me." Pastor Whocares looked at her with disapproval on his face as he began to speak. "Do not get started, because it is not the time or the place. We just stopped by to visit with Mother for a little while and that is all." The first lady mumbled something under her breath, then put a sheepish smile on her face. Normally Mother would have had something to say, but she ignored the first lady and told her and the pastor to have a seat. She told them, "I'm about to fix myself some lunch. Can I fix my pastor and first lady something?" Immediately the pastor replied as they sat down. He said, "I could eat something. Do you want anything, honey?" The first lady looked at her husband and tried to say with her facial expression, *What are you doing?* But he ignored her. She told Mother Rongway, "No thank you. I do not want you to go to any trouble just because of us."

Mother Rongway was still talking in her sweet, motherly voice as she replied, "It will be no trouble at all for my pastor and first lady. I will be glad to do it." Pastor Whocares spoke up and told Mother, "Me and the first lady will have something because we did not have lunch yet, and I am a little hungry." Mother Rongway went out of the room, and the pastor and first lady began to talk. It was clear that the first lady was upset. First Lady Whocares, whose first name was Shirley, was raised in a middle-class family. She was the only child and was raised a little spoiled, but not rotten, and a bit naive. Her parents kept her sheltered from the hardships of the world. She never went hungry, and she did not know what struggling was. Her life was always mapped out for her; she knew what college she was going to at a young age because her parents told her so. She did everything her parents told her because she knew no other way. When she fell in love with a man she met in college and married him without her parents' permission, she quickly learned the true meaning of the word *struggling*. She was taken out of the family's will and excommunicated by friends and family members. Pastor Whocares was all that she had, and finding enough money to pay bills was always a problem.

She asked her husband what was wrong with him. She reminded him, "I told you a hundred times I do not like to eat at your church members' houses." She said, "They cook all that weird stuff. Even the peas have black eyes, and something is wrong when the peas have black eyes." Pastor Whocares looked at her with confusion on his face and asked, "What do you mean *my* members?" He told her, "The church members belong to the Lord, not me, and if you would cook more at home, we would not have to eat at the church members' houses." She looked at him and told him, "Don't start with me." She continued, "Since we are talking, there are a few things I need to get off my chest. You need to tell your church members to stop coming to me with their petty little problems. I have enough problems of my own. I do not want to hear their problems." The pastor looked at her and said, "That is our job. We listen to people's problems and do whatever we can to help them out." She said to him, "That may be *your* job, but that is definitely not *my* job." Then she asked him, "Do I look like a certified counselor to you?" She went on to say, "I told you from day one I did not want to be no first lady, but you just had to be a pastor."

Pastor Whocares stood up, stuck out his chest, proudly strutted around, and said, "I am a rather good pastor if I have to say so myself." But Shirley disagreed and told him, "You are nothing but Mother Rongway's puppet. If Mother tells you to jump, you jump. If she tells you to dance, you dance. If she tells you to talk, you talk. And if she tells you to shut up, you will shut up." Pastor Whocares got upset and tried to express his manhood. He told Shirley, "You know that is not true. I am my own man, and nobody controls me; nobody tells me what to do." Shirley began to laugh and told him, "I made a mistake. I should have said *puppy*. If Mother says bark, you will bark; if she says beg, you will beg; if she says roll over, you will roll over; and if she says fetch, you will fetch. Everybody knows that Mother Rongway runs the church." Pastor Whocares looked at her and told her, "If that is the way you feel, you should pack your bags and go back home to your mother's house." Now that got the first lady's attention. She had to think about things for a minute. She said, "Although it is true that I do not care anything about the people in this backwoods town, there are a few good benefits to being here. Since we have the nicest house in town; do not have to pay any rent or light, water, phone, or cable bill; and do not have to buy groceries, I would be crazy to give all that up." Then Pastor Whocares said, "Not to mention the new car we get every year and that nice big check I get every week, and I sure do not hear you complaining about those furs you got."

So, Shirley admitted that the benefits were nice, but still said, "I just do not like the people, and if Mother Rongway is going to tell you what to do and how to run the church, then she should be the pastor." At that point, the pastor sat back down. He told her, "You need to keep your voice down. Mother Rongway might hear you. I know what is going on. The reason I let Mother have her way is because she controls the money." So, the first lady said to him, "If I am to understand you right, you are saying that you are just acting like a grasshopper so Mother will not cut off your money, but in reality, you are a giant." He agreed and said, "That sums it up, because there is more to me than meets the eye." The first lady was not buying it. She told him, "You are full of turkey, and if you were a giant, we would never have come to this broke-down old town in the first place. You need to admit that you do not have a backbone." Now that really struck a nerve. The pastor firmly told her that was enough. He said, "I must take that kind of talk coming from Mother Rongway, but I do not have to take it from my own wife. I do not particularly like the people in this town myself, but this is the best paying job I ever had. I will kiss up to whomever I have to kiss up to in order to keep it." Now you must understand that Pastor Whocares, whose first name was Clyde, had had a hard life. All his life he'd had to fight. Like his wife, he was an only child. His father was a diligent worker and did everything in his power to support his family and give them a good life. His father had big dreams that never came true, for he died a young man, and his mother died soon after of a broken heart. He was eighteen when he lost both parents, but he was strong and determined to fulfill his dreams. He went to college and got a degree in management. He was a diligent worker like his father before him, but at every job he had, he never could reach his dream of prosperity. He was always overlooked, underpaid, rejected, or neglected. He had to train people to be his boss, even if he was more qualified for the position. He and his wife were middle-class, but money was tight, and he wanted more.

The first lady was still trying to understand his reasoning. She asked him, "Are you saying that we must stay here with a bunch of people we do not like, and you be Mother Rongway's whipping boy, because the money is good?" He reminded her, "You said you like the benefits, and I do not know of any other job that has all these benefits." But First Lady Whocares still was not satisfied, so she asked him, "What about your pride and dignity? How low are you willing to go, and how much longer are you going to put me through this?" All Pastor Whocares could see were dollar signs. He told her, "I will go as low as I must go, because I am not giving up this money. You need to smile and act like you love these people to death. When Mother offered me the job, I said yes." This little revelation caught the first lady by surprise. She asked him, "Are you saying that Mother Rongway hired you and not the deacon board or the members?" He said to her, "I thought you knew that Mother Rongway owns the church, and that her family founded it and set it up." He continued, "After her father, Bishop Rongway, died and left her the church, she needed a pastor, and that was where I came in."

Hearing this really upset First Lady Whocares. She jumped up and began to talk loudly with fear and panic in her voice. She began to say to him, "We are going to hell. You are pastoring a church being run by the devil. Mother Rongway knows the devil personally." Pastor Whocares stood up, walked over to where she was standing, put his hand on her shoulder, and told her, "You need to calm down, because Mother might hear you. You are getting yourself all worked up over nothing. All we must do is play Mother's little games, and we will be fine." But the first lady was really upset and told him, "I do not want to calm down, and I do not want to play Mother's little games. I thought we were working for the Lord, not Mother Rongway." The pastor tried to console her and reminded her, "The Bible does say that the Lord works in mysterious ways. It could be that the Lord is using Mother and we just do not see it." The first lady agreed and said, "Mother Rongway is being used all right, but it is not by the Lord. If you cannot see that, then you need to go back and get a refill, because your religion is as weak as Kool-Aid." At that moment, Mother Rongway came back into the room with a tray of food and drinks, and the pastor and the first lady sat back down. Mother Rongway and First Lady Whocares could not stand one another; they just tolerated each other as much as possible.

Mother put the tray down on one of the end tables and began to serve Pastor Whocares, not bothering to serve the first lady anything. Mother sat down and said, "I'm sorry it took me so long, but I was on the phone with Mother Runnamouth, and you both know how hard it is to get that woman off the phone." The pastor told her that it was not a problem. He said, "Shirley and I were just sitting here talking about how the Lord is using you at the church." The first lady agreed that Mother was being used. Sarcastically, and with a smile on her face, she told Mother, "I have not seen anybody being used like you in a long time." Mother certainly knew how to play her role. Using her sweet, motherly voice, she said, "That means so much to me coming from my pastor and my first lady. I try to live every day so the Lord can use me anytime and anywhere." The first lady turned her head away and said in a muffled voice, "Yeah, you are being used, all right." Now, Mother had incredibly good hearing, so she asked the first lady what she had said. Mother said to her, "You seem to be upset about something. Is there anything wrong?" Pastor Whocares spoke up immediately and told Mother, "Don't pay any attention to Shirley, because she is not feeling her best."

He stood up, put his plate down, and asked Shirley if he could see her outside for a minute. He said to Mother Rongway, "Excuse us for just a moment." Mother replied, "Of course, Pastor. Take your time." The pastor and the first lady went outside. Mother Rongway said to herself, "Thank God the pastor took the first lady outside, because she was about to make me lose my religion." After a few minutes, the pastor and the first lady came back inside. He assured Mother that everything was fine. Mother said, "Okay, then. I hope the first lady feels better. If there is anything I can do, all the first lady must do is let me know." Once again, the pastor said, "The first lady is fine. In fact, we both are fine. We are here in your beautiful house just enjoying the fellowship." Mother told them, "Like I said before, you both mean so much to me. I am so glad that you are my pastor." Pastor told Mother, "The fellowship is great, but I just remembered we have another appointment." He thanked her for the lunch, and they stood up to leave. Mother told them they did not have to rush off. She said, "Some of the other saints are stopping by, and we are going to sit around and talk and have some refreshments and enjoy the fellowship." But the first lady had had all she could tolerate, so she spoke up quickly and said, "Oh, no, we must leave because we have already been here too long. We have places to go and things to do."

If you could not tell, she could not wait to get out of that house. With a cheap grin on her face, Mother Rongway told them, "I'm so glad you two came to see me, because it is always such a pleasure to have my pastor and the first lady in my house." Pastor Whocares said, "It was our pleasure being here because you are such an inspiration to the whole church. I am really glad you are the mother of the church." The first lady had to get in one more jab before they left. She told Mother, "Yes, you are such an inspiration, and I do not know how the church would run without you." Mother told her, "I just do whatever I can to help the church run smoothly." The first lady smiled at Mother, then spoke in an extremely muffled voice and said, "Yes, you run things, all right." Mother was sharp, and nothing went over her head, so she asked the first lady to repeat what she had said. Pastor Whocares stepped in quickly once more and told Mother, "It was nothing, and Shirley was just kidding." He told her they would see her later and hurried his wife out the door. Mother was relieved that they left. She said to herself, "Thank God. I thought they would never leave. That first lady was starting to get on my nerves. She was about to make me mad."

CHAPTER 3

MOTHER'S THREE FAVORITE GIRLS STOPPED BY TO GOSSIP

Mother Rongway resumed tidying up the room when the doorbell rang again. She went to the door and opened it. It was the other saints, Mother Runnamouth, Evangelist Trying, and Missionary Scareaway. She greeted them and told them they were three of her favorite people. She told them to come on in. They all came in, spoke, and hugged. Mother Runnamouth was excited as they all sat down. She said to Mother Rongway, "I could not wait to get to your house, because you started telling me something on the phone about Deacon Aintwright, and it sounded juicy." Mother Runnamouth was the daughter of very wealthy socialites. Her father was a successful doctor, and her mother was the founder of many nonprofit organizations around the world. She was spoiled rotten, arrogant, hateful, and rude. She cared for no one's feelings but her own, and never had to say "I'm sorry" to anyone. From the day she was born, she was reminded of who she was in society. She looked down on everyone and thought extraordinarily little of people who were not in her social circle. Gossip had always been the norm in her family; after all. Her daddy owned half the newspaper company, and they got first dibs on the "real stories" that were never printed. Her parents picked out the richest man for her to marry, but she became unhappy in her marriage, so she got a divorce.

She would never give up her wealthy status or risk her reputation. God forbid if anyone gossiped about her; heads would roll.

Missionary Scareaway was also excited and said, "I also want to hear something juicy. I have not heard any good gossip in a long time, so let the dirt fly." But Mother Rongway told the two of them they needed to hold up a minute. She said, "First, we need to talk to Evangelist Trying; we need to educate her about a few things." Evangelist Trying said, "Mother Rongway is right. I do not know much about the people or the pastor and the first lady since I have been a member of the church for only about a month." Missionary Scareaway told Evangelist Trying, "That is exactly our point. You need somebody to help you get settled in and guide you around the obstacles." Then Mother Runnamouth told her, "That is what we want to do for you, because you are such a sweet person, and we do not want to see you get in with the wrong people and get caught up in some of their mess." Mother Rongway agreed and said, "There is a lot of mess in the church, and I've been here since I was a little girl, and I've seen it all." So, the evangelist humbly said to Mother Rongway, "If you are willing to take the time to be my mentor, then I am willing to do whatever you think is best. After all, I know the mother of the church will not steer me wrong."

Shaking her head, Mother Rongway told her, "Of course not. I will never tell you anything that is not for your own good." Mother Runnamouth quickly agreed and told the evangelist, "Mother Rongway is right. When we first came to the church, Mother Rongway took Missionary Scareaway and I under her wings, and thanks to her, we are who we are today." Missionary Scareaway nodded her head in agreement and said, "I know that is right. When I first came to the church, I was just like you, Evangelist—I trusted everybody. I thought everybody liked me; then, Mother Rongway pulled me to the side and schooled me, and I will forever be in her debt for that." Mother Runnamouth agreed and said, "I was just like the missionary when I first came to the church—I was a sucker for what I thought was love. I will never forget how Mother Rongway took me out to lunch and set me on the right track." Then she told the evangelist, "If you follow Mother Rongway, you will not go wrong."

Evangelist Trying was touched almost to tears as she began to talk. "I just thank God that I found three wonderful, godly women like you three. I am so glad you all see something in me that drew you to little ole me." Mother Rongway told her not to go getting all emotional. She said, "That is my calling—to help people get on the right path before they head off in the wrong direction or get mixed up with the wrong crowd." Now, Missionary Scareaway wanted to get back to why they came to Mother's house in the first place. She said, "Now that evangelist Trying is one of us, I want to know what the juicy gossip about Deacon Aintwright is. I cannot wait any longer, Mother Rongway, so go on and spill the beans." Mother Runnamouth said, "Yeah, Mother Rongway, you have kept us in suspense long enough, so you need to tell us the scoop on Deacon Aintwright." Mother was an expert at lying. She said to them, "You all know I am not the one to start mess, so you all must promise me to keep what I am about to tell you three to yourselves." Mother Runnamouth told Mother Rongway, "You know that the missionary and I do not gossip, and now that the evangelist knows the deal, I believe she will be just like us." Evangelist Trying agreed and said to Mother, "You do not have to worry about me because my lips are sealed."

Mother Rongway continued with her story. She began to tell them, "This morning Deacon Aintwright stopped by to talk. He said he lost his job and was feeling bad and needed someone to talk to. You all know me and know I will listen to anybody's problems and try to help them if I can." Missionary Scareaway agreed and said, "That is just the kind of person you are. You are the type of mother who tries to help everybody." Mother Rongway continued to talk. She told them, "I found out that Deacon Aintwright was dipping into the church's treasure, so I confronted him about it." Mother Runnamouth, Evangelist Trying, and Missionary Scareaway were all surprised by what they just heard. They could not believe Deacon Aintwright would do something like that. Mother Runnamouth was now most surprised. She said, "Oh, Lord, not

Deacon Aintwright. I thought he was an all-right deacon." Evangelist Trying said, "Wow, some people really are not what they appear to be." Then Mother Rongway told them, "Wait. You all have not heard the good part yet. When I confronted him about the money, at first he tried to deny it. Then after he saw he could not get off the hook, you all will not believe what he did next." Missionary Scareaway said, "If he was stealing from the church, I bet he offered to cut you in on the loot to keep you quiet." Mother Rongway said, "I wish, but that was not the case. That low-down, dirty scoundrel tried to proposition me."

Mother Rongway went into her fake crying act to make her story more convincing—and it worked. Now these three sisters were more than surprised; they were shocked. And all three responded in one loud voice, "What?" Mother Rongway continued and said, "He told me he knew I was a lonely woman since my husband died, and that if I kept quiet about the money, he would stop by about once a month to ease my loneliness." Mother Runnamouth, holding her head in her hands, said, "I feel like I'm about to faint." Now Evangelist Trying was still in disbelief. She said, "I thought I had heard it all, but this takes the cake." Missionary Scareaway said, Hold up, because I know you all cannot be talking about the Deacon Aintwright who we all look to as a leader. Listening to you, Mother Rongway, this man has got problems." Then she said to Mother, "Hold up, you said Deacon Rongway is dead. I remember you told me and Mother Runnamouth he went to visit his sister." As always, Mother Rongway had an answer. She said of course, in her sweet, motherly voice, "Deacon Aintwright got me so upset, I did not know what I was saying." She continued, "I meant to say since Deacon Rongway's been away, and you all know me—I do not lie. That is exactly what happened."

So, Mother Runnamouth asked, "What did you say to him after that? I hope you told him off." Mother Rongway kept her lie going and told them, "You all know I did. I told him I was not that kind of woman, and if he did not pay the church back the money he took, I would have him put in jail." Evangelist Trying was still in disbelief and said, "I can see the headlines: 'Well-known deacon, from a well-known church, arrested for embezzling funds from his own church.'" Missionary Scareaway wanted to know what Deacon Aintwright had to say after that. "I bet he was ready to tuck his tail between his legs and run like a dog." Mother Rongway told her, "Not exactly. About that time, his wife, Sister Aintwright, stopped by, and I had to act like nothing happened. I did not see any reason to upset her." Mother Runnamouth said, "I feel so bad for poor Sister Aintwright, married to a crooked deacon. That is why I am not married today. Too many worthless, sorry, crooked, jelly back…" Evangelist Trying cut her off before she could finish her statement. She said to her, "Easy, Mother Runnamouth, I am still looking for a husband. Some of us women are still willing to take a chance."

Missionary Scareaway agreed and said, "I know that is right. There must be a few good brothers out there somewhere, and I want myself one." Mother Rongway told them, "If you two want a husband, that is your choice. All a man can do for me now is what I tell him to do, and nothing else." Missionary Scareaway changed the subject. She said, "Speaking of brothers, that Elder Backnibbler is one strange-acting brother, and Sister Backnibbler is a certifiable fruitcake." They all laughed. Mother Runnamouth, still laughing, said, "I thought I was the only one who noticed. Do you all know who else's elevator does not go all the way to the top? Brother and Sister Liketalie." They were still laughing. Mother Rongway told them, "You all need to stop. Them folks cannot help it if they flew over the cuckoo's nest twice." They kept laughing. Evangelist Trying, still chuckling, said, "From what I can see, about everybody in this church needs to see a psychiatrist." At that moment, the evangelist stopped laughing and realized that everybody else had stopped laughing and was now looking at her. She quickly realized she had messed up and said, "I meant everybody except you three, of course."

The mood in the room changed, and Mother Rongway changed the tone of her voice. She told the evangelist, "I am glad you straightened out that statement. I would hate it if I had to body-slam you." Mother Runnamouth agreed and said, "I sure don't like being called crazy." Missionary Scareaway said, "I do not like being called crazy either. I would hate to have to flip out up in Mother Rongway's house." Missionary Scareaway was raised by a single mom in a dangerous project apartment. She was the oldest of seven siblings. She was sexually abused by her mother's boyfriend, who would get her mother high until she passed out and beat her brothers if they tried to interfere. When her mother died, she and her siblings were separated and placed in foster care. She never saw her siblings again. She had extremely low self-esteem and spent most of her adult life looking for love in all the wrong places.

So, Evangelist Trying, surprised by their reactions, said, "I did not mean to strike a nerve." Evangelist Trying was also raised by a single parent. Her father died when she was two-years-old. Well, that was what her mother had told her. She and her mother had been through a lot. She considered her mother her best friend; her entire world revolved around her mother. She took care of her mother, paid her mother's bills, financed her mother's summer vacations, and did whatever else her mother wanted. She gave up her youth to support her mother, because she felt her mother had given up her youth to support her. Mother Rongway replied in her sweet, motherly voice and said, "Everything is all right, but just do not let it happen again." The evangelist quickly agreed that she would not make that mistake again. The mood changed again, and Mother Rongway asked if the three of them would go to the store for her. She said, "I'm expecting some more company, and I need a few more things." Mother Runnamouth said, "Of course. It will be our pleasure." Missionary Scareaway said, "Mother Rongway, you know I will do anything you ask me to do. All you need to do is just ask." So, Mother Rongway asked the evangelist, "Are you one of my girls?" The evangelist replied, "Of course. I will do whatever you need me to do." Mother Rongway gave them some money and a list of what she needed from the store, and the three of them got up and left.

CHAPTER 4

<u>Mother's Lies Causes Trouble Between the Church Members</u>

Mother Rongway got up and began to straighten up the room, but before she could do much the doorbell rang again. She went to the door, smiling and excited. She opened the door, and it was Elder and Sister Backnibbler. She said to them, "Praise the Lord," and told them to come on in. They both said "Praise the Lord" as they came into the house. Sister Backnibbler asked, "How is my favorite mother doing?" Mother Rongway replied and said, "I'm doing fine," then asked how the two of them were doing. The elder said, "We are doing great, and it was so nice of you to invite us over to your house. We are so honored that you would even think about us." Using her sweet, motherly voice, Mother Rongway said to them, "Out of all the people at the church, you and Sister Backnibbler are my two favorite people." The Backnibblers were both surprised. Sister Backnibbler, smiling, told Mother, "We never knew you felt that way about us. That makes us feel so special." The elder agreed and told Mother, "You are very special to us too." Mother smiled and told them to sit down. She said, "Mother Runnamouth, Missionary Scareaway, and Evangelist Trying went to the store and should be back in a little while." They all sat down. Then, in a serious tone, Mother Rongway said, "Before they get back, I need to talk to you two about something." The elder told her, "Sure thing. We are listening." Sister Backnibbler said to Mother, "You sound troubled. Is everything all right?" Mother Rongway stood up, began to walk around shaking her head, and got into a serious mood. She said to them, "You both know I am not one to start trouble, but I had a terrible experience this morning, and I need someone I can talk to who I can trust." Sister Backnibbler stood up and walked over to Mother and put her hand on Mother's shoulder to comfort her. She told Mother, "You should know you can trust us. Whatever it is, it will not go any farther than this room we are standing in." The elder, now standing, agreed and said, "My wife is right. Whatever you talk to us about will stay between us."

Mother told them they needed to sit back down because what she had to say was not pretty. They all sat back down, and Mother began to talk. She told them, "Earlier today, Deacon Aintwright stopped by. He said he lost his job and needed somebody to whom he could talk." The elder interrupted and said, "Knowing you, I bet you was willing to do all you could to help him." Mother said, "Yes, I was, but that was not the issue," and she continued to talk. She told them, "The deacon began to tell me that he and Sister Aintwright are having some problems at home, and he is not happy. Then, before I knew what was happening, he tried to force himself on me." She pretended to cry to make her story more believable. Sister Backnibbler was outraged. She said, "I cannot believe what I am hearing. This cannot be real." She told Mother Rongway, "I know you do not lie, but this kind of stuff does not happen in the church."

Sister Backnibbler became a famous model at the age of three. Her mother, father, and three older brothers relied on her success. She never saw a dime of her money, and by the time she was eighteen, all the family riches were gone. She became bitter and tried to get back into modeling or movies, but she was told she was too old; a "has-been" by eighteen-years-old. Now broke, she felt she only had one choice: get married. So, she got married and disowned her family, never to see them again. To her, Mother Rongway was an angel.

When the elder heard what Mother had to tell them, he got upset. He said, "I was sitting here trying to keep my cool, but right now my blood is boiling. I have known Deacon Aintwright for years, and no one could have ever made me believe he would do something like that." At that point, Mother Rongway was really putting on her crying show. She told them, "You two will have to excuse me for a few minutes. I need to go wash my face and get myself together." She got up to leave the room. Sister Backnibbler told her, "Take your time Mother. Me and Jethro are in no hurry to leave." Jethro agreed and asked Mother as she went out the room, "Will you fix me a snack if you do not mind? I am hungry." Sister Backnibbler stood up, walked over to where he was sitting, and punched him on the shoulder. She was upset and asked him, "What have I told you about begging? It is getting to the point that I am embarrassed to go anywhere with you." He said to her, "If you would learn how to cook, I would not have to beg for food everywhere we go." He stood up and walked away. She said to him, "If you want to eat every day, then you need to learn how to cook or make yourself a sign that says: 'will work for food.'"

Then he told her, "If you keep on talking junk, I will take you back to your mother's house, where I found you barefooted and nappy headed." She said to him, "You know I am the best thing that ever happened to you. When we first met, you looked a mess, and you still do." He said to her, "Whatever." Then he asked her, "Do you believe all that stuff Mother Rongway was telling us?" Sister Backnibbler said, "Of course I believe Mother Rongway. She is a godly woman if I ever saw one. I know Mother does not lie." The elder disagreed. He said, "Mother Rongway has about as much religion as a tree stump. If it would cost Mother a nickel to stay on the ground and tell the truth, she would rather spend a dollar and climb a tree to tell a lie." Sister Backnibbler laughed and said, "If that is the way you feel, maybe you should straighten Mother out and put her in her place." The elder held up both hands and said, "Oh no, not me. I know better than to cross Mother Rongway." Sister Backnibbler laughed again and said to him,

"Well, then, I suggest you keep your mouth shut, because every time you open it, your brain leaks out."

Elder Backnibbler was raised by his father after his mother died giving birth to him. His father was depressed all the time and never spent any time with him. Though his father never remarried, he had plenty of lady friends. He raised Elder Backnibbler as well as could, but the elder grew up very timid and insecure. He graduated high school and got a trade cutting hair. He became a barber and met his wife modeling at a local hair show.

Mother Rongway came back into the room, and they all sat back down. Mother said, "I am sorry it took me so long, but I was on the phone with Missionary Scareaway. They cannot seem to do anything without me." Then she continued, "What were we talking about before I went out?" Sister Backnibbler reminded her and said, "You was telling us how Deacon Aintwright tried to force himself on you." Mother said, "Yes, now I remember." Then she told them, "Not only did the deacon try to force himself on me, but I found out that he had been stealing money from my church." Now that really surprised Sister Backnibbler. She said, "The deacon must have lost his mind." Then she asked Mother, "Did you tell Sister Aintwright and call the police?" Mother told her, "Neither one. About that time, Sister Aintwright rang the doorbell, and I think that was the only thing that saved me. I did not see any reason to say anything to Sister Aintwright because you both know I am not one to start any trouble." The elder spoke up and told Mother, "You have more in you than I have in me. Just hearing your story makes me want to go over to the deacon's house and punch his lights out." Sister Backnibbler agreed, and added, "I feel the same way, even though I never was one for violence, even before I was saved."

Mother told them not to worry about it. She said, "The deacon will get what is coming to him in time. You two have other things to worry about right now." This confused the Backnibblers, so Sister Backnibbler asked Mother, "What things? We do not have a clue what you are talking about." Mother said to them, "You both know I'm not one to start trouble, but because you two are so special to me, I feel it will be wrong if I do not say something." The elder could not wait. He said to Mother, "Don't keep us in suspense any longer." Mother agreed but told them, "You guys must promise me that you will not get upset, and that you will not say a word to anybody about what I am about to say," and they both agreed. Mother repeated, "You both know I try to keep mess from spreading, but I feel you two need to know this." She went on to say, "Earlier, Evangelist Trying, Mother Runnamouth, and Missionary Scareaway were talking about you two like you were dogs. I had to make them stop." Sister Backnibbler was not convinced and thought Mother was kidding, but Mother assured her she was not. She said, "The way them three were going on, I thought they had something against you and the elder." But the elder said, "I am not surprised. I always thought those three were trouble from the first time I saw them." Sister Backnibbler was still not buying it. She said, "I know you Mother, and I know you will not lie, but it is hard for me to believe my sisters would talk bad about us like that." But Mother insisted that she was not lying. She said to them, "If I'm lying, I'm flying, and as you can see, I do not have any wings on my back." She showed them her back.

At that moment, the doorbell rang. Mother told the Backnibblers to excuse her and went to the door. It was Mother Runnamouth, Missionary Scareaway, and Evangelist Trying. They all came in. Mother told them she was glad they had made it back. She said, "I was starting to worry about you three." Then in her loving, sweet voice, she said, "Look who is here, Elder and Sister Backnibbler." Missionary Scareaway said, "I'm sorry it took so long, but I did not know Mother Runnamouth was so slow, and Evangelist Trying was just as bad." Evangelist Trying spoke up with an attitude and said, "It was not Mother Runnamouth and I who had to go to three different stores to get the so-called bargains." Mother Runnamouth agreed and said, "And we ended up spending the same amount of money anyway. My feet hurt, and I need to sit down." She found a seat and sat down. Mother Rongway asked them, "Where are you all's manners? Are you three going to speak to the Backnibblers?"

Mother Runnamouth asked the Backnibblers to forgive her. She asked them how they were doing. Although Sister Backnibbler had a tough time believing what Mother told them, she now had an attitude. With a phony grin, she said, "We are fine, and it was nice of you to ask." Then she looked the other way. Missionary Scareaway, wondering what was going on, asked, "Are we missing something? Somebody needs to tell us what is going on." Evangelist Trying agreed and said, "We just got here, and it feels mighty cold in here to me."

Elder Backnibbler still had an attitude. He said, "If some people would do like *The Bible* says, and study to keep their mouths shut, the world would be a lot better." Mother Rongway intervened using her sweet, motherly voice, pretending she had no part in what was going on. She said, "Children, children, that is no way for brothers and sisters in the Lord to act. You all should sit down and relax, and I will fix everyone a snack." The elder told Mother, "Thanks anyway, but me and Sister Backnibbler must leave." Then he turned to his wife and said, "Let us go." They both got up and started for the door, and Sister Backnibbler thanked Mother Rongway for inviting them. She said to her, "I will call you later." Then she told Mother Runnamouth, Missionary Scareaway, and Evangelist Trying, "I will see you three later," as she rolled her eyes and turned her head away from them. They left. Mother Runnamouth looked puzzled and asked Mother Rongway, "What was all that about?" Mother Rongway did not miss a beat. She said, "I have no idea what their problem was. One minute they were fine, and the next minute they started acting funny." Then she smiled, lying through her teeth.

"I must go out for a little while and will be back shortly. I wonder if you guys would mind staying here until I get back, because I am expecting some more company." Missionary Scareaway said, "I do not mind staying. I do not have anywhere else to go or anything to do." Evangelist Trying said, "I don't mind," and Mother Runnamouth told Mother Rongway, "You do not even have to ask me, you know I will be glad to stay." But Mother Rongway told her, "I was hoping you would go with me so we can talk, mother to mother," and she agreed.

Missionary Scareaway looked at Evangelist Trying and told her, "They must have stuff to talk about that they don't want us little people to know about." Mother Rongway assured her that was not the case. She said, "Sometimes us elderly folk need to get together and talk every now and then." The evangelist told Mother Rongway, "We understand, and you two go ahead; we will stay here until you both get back." Mother Rongway thanked them and promised to be back in a little while. They left. Missionary Scareaway went and looked out the window to be sure they had left. She went back and sat down. She then told Evangelist Trying, "I thought they would never leave. Now we can get down to some serious talking." The evangelist looked puzzled and asked her, "What do you mean by some serious talk?" The missionary told her, "I could not say anything around Mother Rongway or Mother Runnamouth, but you need to trust what I am saying. You do not want to be a member of Mother's church, and really, with the emphasis on *really*, you do not want to be one of Mother Rongway's girls." Now the evangelist was a little confused. She reminded the missionary, "Earlier you told me that when you first came to Mother Rongway's church, she took you under her wings and made you who you are today. Isn't that what you said?"

Missionary Scareaway admitted, "That is what I said, but it's more like being under Mother's feet than being under her wings. I don't know if you noticed or not, but Mother Rongway has some big feet." Still confused, the evangelist asked, "If you feel that way, why do you stay under Mother's feet? Why don't you just leave?" The missionary told her, "I wish it were that easy. You do not know the real Mother Rongway, and trust me, you do not want to know the real Mother Rongway." Being naive, the evangelist wanted to know why. "I want to know what is so bad about Mother Rongway. She seems like a nice, sweet mother to me." The missionary agreed and said, "On the outside, Mother Rongway can be the sweetest, nicest person you have ever known, but do not get on her bad side; you will be sorry you did. That is when you will see the real Mother Rongway without the mask." The evangelist was still having a tough time believing what she was hearing. She said to the missionary, "I hear what you are saying, and you know Mother Rongway better than I do, but I don't know if I believe all that." The missionary told her, "If I'm lying, a pig isn't pork." She continued and added, "Pastor and First Lady Whocares are more than a trip; they are a whole journey. I went to talk to the first lady about some stuff I was dealing with and was shocked at what she did and told me to do."

Curious, the evangelist asked what was said. Missionary Scareaway told her, "The first lady gave me a quarter and told me to call somebody who cared." Trying not to laugh too hard, the evangelist told her she must be joking. She said, "First Lady Whocares is one of the sweetest, most caring people I know." The missionary told her, "I feel sorry for you. Evidently you don't know many people." The evangelist said to her, "Very funny, but from what I can see, nobody in this church is what they appear to be. Everybody is jacked up." The atmosphere changed. Missionary Scareaway stood up and walked over to where the evangelist was sitting. In a serious tone of voice, she asked the evangelist, "What is that supposed to mean, and what are you trying to say?" The evangelist, sensing she may have struck a nerve, said, "I was not trying to say anything. I was just making small talk." The missionary said to her, "I hope that was all you were doing, because I would hate to have to take off my weave and get down to business." The evangelist asked her not to take off her weave. She said, "My heart cannot take what the real you might look like." The tension continued building as Missionary Scareaway moved her head from side to side. She told Evangelist Trying, "Everybody tells me how good I look, so you must not know what you are talking about." The evangelist said, "All that proves is, along with everything else, the people in this church need to get their eyes checked."

The missionary said, "For your information, not too long ago, I won first place in a beauty pageant." The evangelist began to really pour fuel on the fire. "The beauty pageant must have been held at the circus because you sure look like a clown to me." By now, the missionary was fuming. She told the evangelist, "you have jokes and must think you are funny." Then she got loud and asked the evangelist, "do you see me laughing?" The evangelist stood up and said, "I am not making jokes, but I tell it the way I see it. My name is Mary Lou Trying, and I am not lying." Now missionary Scareaway was really fired up. She told Evangelist Trying, "I will baptize you on this floor, and I think that would be really funny." But Evangelist Trying did not back down. She told the missionary, "Do not take my meekness for weakness. I will cast them demons out of you or cut them out; it does not matter to me which one." By this time, you could almost see smoke coming out of Missionary Scareaway's ears. With both fists balled up, she told Evangelist Trying, "You need a good, sanctified whipping, and it just so happens I'm feeling the spirit at this very moment." Just then, the doorbell rang. She said to the evangelist, "Saved by the bell. Are you going to get that?" Evangelist Trying rolled her eyes and said, "I guess I will, but I didn't know I was the door person."

She went and opened the door, and it was Brother and Sister Liketalie. They both spoke to her, and she responded in a profoundly serious tone of voice to come in. Then she went across the room, away from Missionary Scareaway, and sat down. Missionary Scareaway continued to speak to the Liketalies in a serious tone and moved as far away from Evangelist Trying as she could get and sat down. The Liketalies had no clue what they just walked into. Sister Liketalie was excited to see them, so she spoke cheerfully and said, "I have not seen you two in a long time. How are you folks doing?" Brother Liketalie agreed and said, "We missed seeing you two" with a sheepish smile on his face.

Brother Liketalie's father was a successful lawyer, and his mother was a stay-at-home mom. Life was easy for him. His father would take him to different women's houses and introduce their kids as his sisters and brothers. His father had several families and would lie to his mom about taking him to baseball and football games during those visits; he even made him lie to his mother about the times they spent together at other women's houses. As he got older, he became very crafty at lying.

He was a womanizer and had several girlfriends at one time that knew nothing of each other. He was a party animal and would party all week long. He finally went to college and became a lawyer like his father, and his father made him a partner at his law firm. His father died a few years later and left the firm to him. He was always driving the streets to find quick love, and one day he found his wife—the last one of many.

Evangelist Trying very sarcastically told them, "You guys have not missed anything by not seeing the missionary," then smiled with a fake smile. Then, in a sweet, calm voice, Mission Scareaway asked the Liketalies, "Would one of you lay hands on me and pray?" Sister Liketalie was concerned, so she asked the missionary, "Are you sick or something?" She walked over to where Missionary Scareaway was sitting and felt her head to see if she had a fever. In a sweet voice, the missionary told her, "No, I'm not sick." Then, with a loud, angry voice, she yelled, "I have murder on my mind, and I need prayer before I body-slam somebody!" Evangelist Trying, in a calm voice, said, "I don't know who the missionary thinks she can body-slam, but if she thinks she can body-slam me, then you should pray for her beforehand, because it will be too late to pray for her later." Brother Liketalie was shocked. He told them, "Hold up. You two sound like you are about ready to throw down. I do not know what the problem is, but I am sure that two saved, anointed women of God like you two can work it out."

Missionary Scareaway, being the rotten, arrogant, hateful, rude person that she was, told Brother Liketalie, "You are so right." She pretended to apologize to Evangelist Trying, then said, "I agree with you, Brother Liketalie, when you say I am a saved and anointed woman of God." Evangelist Trying looked at her in awe. She said to her, "You must be a real, live magician, because one minute you are a saint, then the next minute you are a demon, then the next minute you are a saint again. One of these days, you must show me how you do that." Sister Liketalie told them, "I think you both need a time-out. It is not right for two sisters in the Lord to be acting like this." Brother Liketalie agreed and asked them, "What would Mother Rongway say if she were here?" Missionary Scareaway agreed and told him, "Once again you are right. This is Mother's house, and we should not be acting this way in her house, so I'm leaving." She got up to leave. Sister Liketalie told her, "You do not have to leave. Mother Rongway should be back soon, and I'm sure she can help you and the evangelist work out whatever the problem is." Evangelist Trying agreed with Sister Liketalie and told the missionary, "You don't have to leave, because I'm leaving." She got up, and they both started toward the door. Sister Liketalie tried to stop them from leaving, but their minds were made up, so they left.

Brother Liketalie told her, "It is all right. Just let them go. There was not anything we could have done to change their minds." Sister Liketalie asked Brother Liketalie, "Do you have any idea what that was about? I have never seen them act like that before." Brother Liketalie said, "I do not have a clue. It must be a full moon or something. Some people act funny when the moon changes." They both sat down, wondering what had just happened.

CHAPTER 5

Mother's Lies Brought Everyone to Their Boiling Point

A few minutes had passed when Mother Rongway and Mother Runnamouth came in. Mother Rongway, in a cheerful mood, announced their return and asked if anyone had missed them. They took the bags into the kitchen and came back into the living room and sat down. She looked around for Missionary Scareaway and Evangelist Trying and asked, "Where are my girls? Did they already leave?" Sister Liketalie told her, "Yes, they left, and when me and Bubba got here, the two of them were at each other's throat. They were about to throw down." Brother Liketalie agreed and told her, "You have never lied. I thought it was about to be Ali and Frazier all over again." He threw a few punches. Mother Runnamouth was a little upset that she had missed it. She said, "I knew I should have stayed here. I always miss the good stuff." Mother Rongway told her, "You need to stop. You should know by now that those two got mental problems." Mother Runnamouth agreed and said, "I forgot about that. If you be a around them for any length of time, you can tell." Sister Liketalie disagreed. She said, "I'm around the evangelist and the missionary a lot, and they both seem perfectly normal to me." Brother Liketalie said, "I do not believe that either. I know those two do not have any mental problems."

Mother Rongway asked Brother Liketalie, "What would you know about normal? Is not your Mother in the crazy house." Mother

Runnamouth perked up like a baby bird with its mouth open waiting for the worm. She snapped her finger and said, "I haven't heard about that." Then she told Mother Rongway, "Go ahead and preach the gospel." Sister Liketalie tried to defend her husband and told Mother Rongway, "Hold up, you know Bubba is sensitive about his family." Maybe sister Liketalie thought that would stop Mother from saying anything else, but she was wrong. Mother looked at her, and in her sweet, motherly voice, she asked Sister Liketalie, "How are your drunk stepfather and your drugged-out stepmother doing?" Sister Liketalie jumped up, put both hands on her hips, her head moving from side to side, and said to Mother, "I know you did not go there. I know you are old, but I am not afraid to fight an old woman."

Sister Liketalie was given up at birth. She never knew who her real parents were. She was abused in foster homes all her life. She had to lie to DCFS about her treatment in the foster homes, which made her bitter and confused. She was never adopted. When she was old enough to leave the abusive homes, she checked herself into a shelter for abused women. She sold drugs, smoked, and sold her body just to survive. She learned how to fight at an early age. One day she was walking the streets and the man she would later marry picked her up and told her she could have a better life. He took her to a drug rehab center, got her cleaned up, and married her.

Brother Liketalie tried to calm her down and told her to let it go. He said, "Mother Rongway sounds like the one who has the problems." Mother Runnamouth tried to get in on the action. She jumped up, balled up her fists, and told Mother Rongway, "Let me take care of your light work. I have been working out." Mother Rongway told her, "That will not be necessary." Mother Runnamouth sat back down. Mother Rongway then turned to Brother and Sister Liketalie and told them, "You both know you have problems, I know you have problems, and now Mother Runnamouth knows you have problems, so let's just leave it at that." Sister Liketalie agreed but said, "I do not want our business in the streets. Make sure it does not go any further than this room." Mother Rongway told her, "Of course it will not go any further. Everyone knows I am not the one to start no mess." Mother Runnamouth told Mother Rongway, "I am glad you stopped me a few minutes ago; I might have hurt somebody. I know karate, and my hands are lethal weapons." She held up her hands for Mother to see. Mother Rongway laughed and told her, "Okay, if you say so, but personally I think your mouth is a lethal weapon, but that's just my opinion."

Mother Runnamouth developed an attitude and said to Mother Rongway, "You done went too far. Remember, I can go in your closet and pull out some dirt that will curl Sister Liketalie's weave." Mother Rongway told her to calm down. She said, "I was just kidding. Come into the kitchen and give me a hand." Mother Runnamouth said, "That's more like it. I did not want to have to go down that dirty road again." She told them they would be back. They got up and left the room. Brother Liketalie began to talk with his wife. He said to her, "Maybe it's just me, but I feel those two old mothers need to be put in a rest home somewhere." Sister Liketalie disagreed. "I think they need to be put in a mental institution. I do not trust Mother Rongway." Brother Liketalie laughed and agreed with her. He went on to say, "I do not trust Mother Rongway either. There is something about that woman that just does not seem right." Sister Liketalie told him there was not anything right about that woman. She said, "*The Bible* says that the devil is the father of all lies, and Mother Rongway must be his sister."

Brother Liketalie was not the sharpest tool in the toolbox. He began to laugh and tell her, "Flesh and blood did not reveal that to you. I am sure you must have ESPN." Now it took sister Liketalie a minute to comprehend what he was trying to say. She told him, "I do not need ESPN to see through Mother Rongway. I do not know how old Mother is, but she has been lying so long she would not know the truth if it walked up to her and slapped that wig off her head." Then she asked him "What is ESPN?" So, he told her, "It means extra special people knowledge, although I am not sure about the word knowledge, if it starts with a K or a N," and once again told her that was what she had. She looked at him smiling, shook her head, and told him, "You have been around Mother Rongway too long. You starting to sound just like her." He told her, "OK, just drop the subject, because I do not want you to get upset because you know you have been sick."

At that moment, the doorbell rang and Brother Liketalie got up to answer it. He opened the door, and it was Deaconess Donothing. He greeted her and told her to come in. She came in and spoke to him and Sister Liketalie. She said, "I did not think anyone would be here at Mother Rongway's house, so maybe I came at an inconvenient time." Sister Liketalie stood up and greeted her and told her, "That's nonsense. It's always a pleasure to see you." Brother Liketalie agreed and said to her, "You are one of our favorite people at the church." The deaconess saw her opportunity. She said to him, "If that is true, let me borrow a hundred dollars. I need to get my hair done and I am between blessings." Sister Liketalie looked at him, laughed, and told him, "You put your foot in your mouth again, so cough up the money." That caught Brother Liketalie off guard. Cheesing, he told the deaconess, "I love you, but I'm between blessings myself." They all sat down and the deaconess said, "I did not think the two of you had any money anyway. You two never give any money in the church offering, and every time there is a free meal at church, you two are always the first two in line."

This struck a nerve with the Liketalies. Brother Liketalie told her, "That is not true. One time, me and Johnnie Sue were second in line. One time we were even third in line." The deaconess said, "I don't remember that, but I do remember the time the two of you ate so much that Mother Rongway told both of you to leave so somebody else could get something to eat." Sister Liketalie told the deaconess, "Okay, we get the point and me and Bubba repented for that. We do not do that anymore." The deaconess told them, "I know you folks do not. Since Mother Rongway threatened to put you two out of her church, you guys straightened right up." Brother Liketalie was surprised by what he was hearing. He asked her, "How do you know about that? We did not tell anyone about that." The deaconess said to him, "Must I remind you, or have you forgotten, whose house you are in? You should know by now that Mother Rongway tells everything about everybody who is a member of her church." Sister Liketalie said to Bubba, "I told you that Mother Rongway has a problem with her mouth, and the problem is, she cannot keep it shut." Bubba agreed and said, "I am not surprised. Mother is like a broke stove; she cannot keep anything." Johnnie Sue paused, shook her head, and said to Bubba, "You must mean a broke refrigerator." Bubba said, "Yes, that is what I meant. I thought that did not sound right."

At that point, the deaconess asked where Mother Rongway was. Bubba told her, "She and Mother Runnamouth are in the kitchen fixing us a snack." Johnnie Sue asked her, "Is there something you need to see Mother about?" The deaconess stood up and said, "In fact, there is. A few months ago, out of the goodness of my heart, I loaned Mother Rongway some big money, and every time I ask her about the money, she just laughs in my face." Bubba, trying to be sympathetic, said, "That is cold, but when you say, 'big money,' just how much money are you talking about?" The deaconess told him, "I don't tell everybody, because I don't want people to know that I have money." She motioned for them to come closer and whispered, "I loaned that woman a whopping ten-dollar bill." At that moment, Brother and Sister Liketalie began to laugh uncontrollably. The deaconess got upset and told them that they needed help. She said, "I bet that if Mother Rongway owed you two money, you would not be laughing." Bubba, still laughing, apologized and told her, "I did not mean to laugh, but you caught me off guard with that one."

Johnnie Sue, still laughing, agreed and said to the deaconess, "When you said, 'big money,' I was expecting you to say five or six hundred dollars." The deaconess told them, "There is no way I would loan Mother Rongway that much money even if I had it. Mother is out of control as it is, and she does not have any money. I cannot even imagine what she would be like if she had that kind of money." Bubba agreed and told her, "You are right. Mother is out of control, but I believe she has plenty of money. Do not forget, she owns the church." Johnnie Sue agreed with Bubba and told them, "That is what I been saying all along, but nobody will believe me." At that moment, the doorbell rang. Brother Liketalie got up and went to the door. He opened the door, and there stood Sister Knowsall and Minister Wannado. He said to them, "Come on in, and how are you two doing?" Minister Wannado, in his wannabe preacher voice, said, "Praise the Lord, my brother and sister." He went on to say, "The Lord is good, and the Lord is blessing me right now."

One thing you must understand about Minister Wannado. He was raised in the church. He knew everything there was to know about church. He came from a lengthy line of pastors; all his ancestors were preachers, and they all pastored a church. His dream was to one day pastor his own church. The problem was that no one had appointed or ordained him to preach. He was self-appointed, and everywhere he went, he was eager and ready to preach a word. He had never been married and never dated very much. For a few years he had had his eyes on sister Knowsall but did not let it be known because he was not sure she felt the same way about him.

Sister Knowsall spoke and said, Praise the Lord to Brother and Sister Liketalie and the Deaconess. How are you all doing?" Sister Liketalie spoke to the two of them and said, "Me and Bubba did not expect to see you two at Mother's house today." Brother Liketalie agreed and commented on the fact that the two of them were together. Then he asked, "What is up with that? Is there anything going on that me and Sister Liketalie and the Deaconess do not know about?" The Deaconess, a little upset to see Minister Wannado and Sister Knowsall together, wanted to know the same thing. Minister Wannado got in his preacher mode and, using his preacher's voice, said to Bubba, "The Lord is keeping me. Although Sister Knowsall is as fine as Ruby Johnson, as gorgeous as Virginia Preston, as magnetic as Betty Harris, as sweet as Alice Crumble..." Sister Knowsall interrupted him before he could go any further and told him, "Bring your mind back in Preacher." Sister Liketalie jumped in and asked him, "What do you know about my friends Ruby Johnson and Virginia Preston and all those other women you named?" Deaconess Donothing, in a sad voice, wanted to know the same thing. She took out a handkerchief and patted her face, then told Minister Wannado, "I did not hear you call my name when you were naming all those other women."

Deaconess Donothing was a mystery. No one knew anything about her background or where she came from. She just showed up at the church one Sunday, and when they gave the invitation to join the church, she did. She was appointed a deaconess right away because Mother Rongway recognized that she was easily manipulated. She was very naive and susceptible to whatever Mother Rongway or anyone else tried to do. She was not "all there" in the commonsense department, but she was hopelessly in love with Minister Wannado, who did not pay her any attention; but that did not discourage her at all. She desperately wanted a husband and had made up her mind that he was the one for her.

Minister Wannado came to himself and asked them to excuse him. He said, "I lost my head for a minute." Then he said, "Sister Knowsall is a nice, sweet, beautiful, kind, lovely sister, but the Lord is keeping me." Brother Liketalie laughed and told Minister Wannado, "I'm praying for you because you sound like you have a few issues." Sister Knowsall agreed and said, "For a minute, I thought the preacher man had lost it." Sister Liketalie agreed and said, "For a minute, I thought the same thing." But the deaconess, as she patted her hair, told Minister Wannado, "Do not pay them any attention. I did not think that at all. In fact, I think you got it going on." Minister Wannado tried to ignore her and told them, "All I am trying to say is those sisters got souls to be saved like everybody else. I am believing that one day the Lord is going to let me get close enough to them to lay hands on them. When I do, I am going to cast out those husbands, oops, I meant those sins. Then they can be with me, oops, I meant they can be free to serve the Lord." Then he told Satan, "Get behind me and get out of my mouth." Brother Liketalie laughed again and said to Minister Wannado, "We all get the point, Preacher. The Lord may be keeping you right now, but we believe that the first chance you get, you would like for someone else to keep you for a while." Minister Wannado got indignant and shouted out, "The devil is a liar," then spoke in somebody's tongue. Then he told them, "The Lord is my shepherd and gives me what I want." Deaconess Donothing got excited and shouted, "Oh, glory, the Lord done heard my prayers! I knew Minister Wannado had his eyes on me all the time." Then she fainted. Of course, everyone ignored her because they knew how she was. Sister Knowsall told Minister Wannado not to get upset. She said, "We were just having some fun. You need to lighten up. You're too stiff." Then she said, "Somebody needs to help me get Deaconess Donothing up off this floor." Sister Liketalie agreed as she helped Sister Knowsall get the deaconess up off the floor. She told the minister, "You need to let your hair down a little. You sound like you are about ready to take a text and preach a sermon." They put the deaconess on the sofa.

Brother Liketalie got excited and told the minister, "Come on and give us a word." Now of course, Minister Wannado never missed an opportunity to put on a show. He said, "I guess I will, because I do not want to disappoint my parishioners." Sister Knowsall sighed and said, "Oh boy, here we go." She told Brother Liketalie he had done it now. She said, "We are in for a full-blown message." Sister Liketalie said, "We better get ready to have some church." At that moment, the deaconess woke up, still a little out of it, and asked, "What happened? I think I fainted. Did Minister Wannado lay his anointed hands on me?" Minister Wannado spoke up and told her, "No, Deaconess, not my holy hands." Then he told them, "Before I get started, I think we all need to take coprunion to cleanse our souls." Brother Liketalie, a little confused, said, "Hold up, Minister. I know what communion is, but I never heard of coprunion." Sister Liketalie agreed and told him, "You got to explain that one." Sister Knowsall agreed and said, "I never heard of coprunion either." The lovesick deaconess said, "I never heard of it either, but whatever Minister Wannado wants me to do, all he got to do is just say the word." They all gave her a look that communicated: *Of course you will.*

Minister Wannado told them, "I am not qualified to do communion, so I do coprunion. Instead of grape juice, I use prune juice. There is not anything like it to cleanse your soul." Brother Liketalie said to him, "I don't mean to rain on your parade, but I think prune juice will cleanse more than our soul." They all agreed. Minister Wannado agreed and said, "You might be right about the prune juice." They high fived each other, then he told them, "We won't do coprunion this time." Sister Knowsall got excited and told him, "Come on and give us a word. Let us have some church up in here." Minister Wannado went into preacher mode and said, "Members of the Rongway First Liberation Church, I would like to take a few minutes of your time, to conversate, not to constipate, but to elaborate, to help you concentrate on the information, about your situation, about your liberation from the sin in the nation." Brother Liketalie jumped up and shouted, "Preach, Wannado, preach." Minister Wannado shouted, "Can I get an *Amen* in the house?"

At that moment, Mother Rongway and Mother Runnamouth came rushing into the room. Mother Rongway got excited and said, "I thought that was Wannado." She said to him, "Preach, boy, preach! Let the Lord use you!" Sister Liketalie told him, "Say the word, Wannado; say it like you know it." Sister Knowsall told him, "Go ahead, preacher man. I'm feeling it." The deaconess agreed and told him, "Go ahead and preach. You are making the hairs stand up on the back of my neck." Minister Wannado continued and said, "When you need a doctor, you call on the Lord. When you need a lawyer, you call on the Lord. When you need a homeboy, you call on the Lord, and he will be right there." Then he asked, "Can I get an *Amen*?" Mother Runnamouth jumped up and told him, "Go ahead and tell it like it is." He continued and said, "Is there anybody here who knows how good God is? God is better than a cold Mountain Dew on a hot summer day. God is better than fried chicken on a Sunday afternoon at Mama's house. God is better than a bowl of rocky road ice cream in the middle of the night." Brother

Liketalie, still standing, told Wannado, "Do not make me shout up in here. I am about ready to cut my step." Sister Knowsall said, "I want to take my weave off and let it all hang out." The deaconess agreed and said, "The way Wannado is preaching makes me feel like breakdancing." Everyone stopped and looked at the deaconess in awe.

Mother Rongway told them not to pay the deaconess any attention. Then she said to Minister Wannado, "Go ahead and come on down Truth Street and let the Lord use you." Minister Wannado continued in his preacher voice and said, "I want to tell you all about the three little Hebrew boys, Shadrach, Meshach, and that other bad negro." Mother Runnamouth told him, "Go on and preach. That is my favorite story." Minister Wannado continued and said, "That first little boy built his house out of straw, and when the big bad wolf came along, he huffed and puffed until he blew his house down." Brother Liketalie, still excited, told Minister Wannado, "That's it! Tell it like you know it. You are preaching now." Minister Wannado continued and said, "Somebody told me that that second little boy built his house out of sticks, and when the big bad wolf came, he huffed and puffed until he blew his house down." Sister Knowsall, confused, told Minister Wannado, "I think you got your stories mixed up, but you are preaching." Minister Wannado told her, "Do not stop me now, because I am on a roll." He went on to say, "But that last little boy, that bad negro, built his house out of bricks. And when that big bad wolf came along, he huffed and he puffed, he huffed and he puffed, but he could not blow his house down."

He continued, "I just want to let you all know you better build your house out of bricks, or that big bad wolf—oops, I meant to say the devil will blow your house down." Then he asked, "Can I get an *Amen* and a *Thank you, Jesus?*" Sister Liketalie told him, "Go ahead and preach, because you know you know the word. I never heard that story preached like that before." Mother Rongway agreed and said, "I'm about ready to cut a step up in here." Then she told him, "Preach, boy." The deaconess told them, "I could have told you all that Minister Wannado was diversified. He can preach the word forward and backward." Minister

Wannado continued and said, "I am getting ready to close, but before I do, I want to let you all know that the Lord will deliver you. The Lord delivered Daniel from the lion's den. He delivered David from Goliath. The Lord will deliver you from diarrhea. Won't He make you clean, inside?" Then he asked, "Can I get an *Amen*, a *Thank you, Jesus*, and a *Hallelujah*?" Mother Rongway said, "That was a word. You should be the pastor of the church." Mother Runnamouth agreed and said, "I know that is right. I do not mean any harm, but Pastor Whocares cannot preach like that." Sister Knowsall agreed and said, "I did not know that Minister Wannado was so gifted in the word." Brother Liketalie, still excited, said, "I could have told you all. Me and Minister Wannado are like brothers, and we are always on the same page. He is my homeboy."

Sister Liketalie slipped up and said, "Yes, they were in jail together a few years ago." Everyone was surprised. Mother Rongway asked Sister Liketalie, "What on earth are you talking about?" Sister Liketalie, realizing what she had done, asked, "Did I say that out loud? I thought I was just thinking it." Deaconess Donothing said to Minister Wannado, "Say that it is not true, because if it is true, it is over between us. I did not know you was a jailbird." Understandably upset, Brother Liketalie asked Johnnie Sue, "How could you do that to me and put my business out like that?" Why don't you just go to the newspaper and take out an ad? If you want to hang out dirty laundry, just remember, I can dig in your laundry basket and find a lot of dirty laundry." Mother Runnamouth, trying to stir things up, walked over to Brother Liketalie and encouraged him to speak the word. She said, "I like doing laundry, but I like it even better when someone else is doing it. Hang it, Brother, and let the dirt fly." Sister Knowsall spoke up, "Hold up. I do not see any reason to take that any further. Everyone does not need to know all your business."

Mother Rongway never missed a chance to stir up some mess. In her sweet, motherly voice, she told Sister Knowsall, "Bless your little heart. How is that little girl your mother keeps, the one you said was your adopted sister?" By then, Sister Knowsall became extremely nervous—and she had reason to be nervous. Mother Rongway had a history of starting a mess, so she asked Mother, "What are you talking about?" Mother Rongway told her, "Come now. I know everything about every member at my church. I just happen to know that the little girl is your daughter, one that you had at an incredibly early age. One that you do not want anybody to know about." The deaconess stood up and said, "I think I will be leaving. It is getting too hot in here for me." Mother Rongway told her, "It is OK, and it is always a pleasure to see you. One of these days, I am going to pay you the money I owe you." She laughed as the deaconess left. Mother Runnamouth was anxious to get back to their discussion. She told Mother Rongway, "Tell us some more, because it was getting better and better." Minister Wannado tried to cool things down. He told them, in his preacher voice, "Don't let the devil drive this car." They all looked at him and they all shouted at the same time and told him to shut up.

Sister Knowsall was almost in tears. She asked Mother Rongway, "How could you do that to me and put my business out like that?" Mother Rongway, in her loving, motherly voice, assured Sister Knowsall that her secret was safe with her. Then she smiled and said, "I just might need you to do me a favor now and then." Sister Liketalie was shocked. She said to Mother Rongway, "I know you are not blackmailing Sister Knowsall? Please tell me that is not what you are doing?" Sister Knowsall sat down holding her head in her hands. She knew she was in trouble and asked the Lord to help her poor little soul. Sister Liketalie was now angry. She told Mother Rongway, "I have seen some low-down, dirty people before, but none like you." Mother Runnamouth had to agree. She told Mother Rongway, "I thought I knew you. Out of all the years we have been friends, I've never seen this side of you." Mother Rongway told them to wake up. She said, "I'm a businesswoman, and I found out that in business, I must know all the angles."

Minister Wannado, again in his preacher voice, began to say, "If I may interject a few words to dissect the problem, that I may redirect your minds, and hopefully you all will find that Mother Rongway is lying." Brother Liketalie said, "I also think Mother Rongway is fabricating, or at least stretching the truth." That struck a nerve with Mother Rongway. She put both hands on her hips, began moving her head from side to side, and with an angry voice said, "Hold up, Brother Paul and Brother Silas," referring to Paul and Silas in the bible. "You two do not know how to act since you got out of jail. If you mess with me, it is going to take more than a prayer at midnight to get you out of jail this time." Sister Knowsall stood up and headed toward the door. She said, "I don't know about anyone else, but I think it's time for me to leave." Sister Liketalie felt the same way and said to Bubba, "I think it is time for us to leave also." Mother Rongway changed back to her sweet, motherly voice and said to them, "Children, children, can't we all just get along?" Minister Wannado spoke up again and told them, "Hold on, children of the highest God. It is clear to see that this poor soul needs prayer. I think we all need to fall down on our knees and pray for this sick-minded, demon-possessed, backbiting, two-faced, lying, hypocritical old woman." Then he moved close to the door to make a quick getaway if he needed to.

You could almost see smoke coming out of Mother Rongway's ears. An excited Mother Runnamouth told them, "You all better move back and give Mother Rongway some room. I think she is about to turn into the hulk." At that moment, before anybody could leave, the doorbell rang. Mother Runnamouth got upset. She said, "Every time I think I'm about to see a good beatdown, the doorbell rings." She went to the door and to her surprise there stood Deacon and Sister Aintwright. The deacon told her, "I was not expecting to see you here." Mother Runnamouth sarcastically said, "I bet you wasn't." She then told Mother Rongway, "The Aintwrights are here." Mother Rongway, in her sweet, motherly voice, spoke and told them, "Come on in. You two know everybody." Everybody spoke. Deacon Aintwright said to Mother Rongway, "We did not know you had company. Maybe we can come back at another time." Mother told him, "That is nonsense.

You and sister Aintwright come on in and sit down. You are two of my favorite people." The deacon laughed and said, "Please take us off that list. We would rather not be your favorite people, if that is okay with you."

Then the doorbell rang again. Once again, Mother Runnamouth went to answer it, complaining that the doorbell kept ringing. "Every time things start to get good, the doorbell rings." She opened the door, and it was the Backnibblers. Sister Backnibbler said, "We did not know you would still be here, but it's good to see you again." Mother Runnamouth spoke and told them to come in. Then she said, "It's beginning to look like we're having a Tupperware party or something," as she sat back down. Mother Rongway told them, "Do not pay any attention to Mother Runnamouth, because she is just old. You all know how crabby old people can get sometimes." She told them to come on in and sit down. Mother Runnamouth, a little upset, told Mother Rongway, "You are not who I would call Mother Charming y." Elder Backnibbler interrupted and said, "Maybe we came at an inconvenient time. We can stop by tomorrow." Mother Rongway said to him, "Do not be silly. I am sure you and Sister Backnibbler have a good reason for stopping by again." Sister Knowsall spoke up and said to them, "If it is personal, I advise you all not to say anything in Mother Rongway's house. Before you know it, your business will be all over town."

Sister Liketalie agreed and told them, "Sister Knowsall isn't lying. You will be better off going on the six o'clock news. Maybe everybody in town will not see the news, but if you say anything in Mother Rongway's house, I guarantee you everybody and their brother will know." The elder, a little confused, said to them, "I do not know what you two mean, but I need to leave anyway. I do not think I can stay in the room with a certain deacon without getting violent." Deacon Aintwright was stunned. He told the elder to hold up. He looked around the room and said, "I am the only deacon in the room, and I know you cannot be talking about me. If you are, and if you want to throw down, you better bring your lunch, because it is going to be an all-day job." He started walking toward the elder, and Sister Aintwright pulled him back. Mother Runnamouth jumped up and said, "That doorbell better not ring." At that moment, the doorbell rang again. She screamed and said, "Will somebody please disconnect that doorbell?" Minister Wannado spoke up and told her, "It is just like the Lord. He even knows when to ring your bell." Then he spoke in somebody's tongue. Mother Runnamouth opened the door, and it was Missionary Scareaway and Evangelist Trying.

The missionary spoke and asked Mother Runnamouth, "Why are you still here?" Mother Runnamouth told her, "I am grown, and it's none of your business anyway." The evangelist spoke and said, "I need to move out of the way. I do not want to get in the way of an out-of-control right hook." Mother Runnamouth assured her, "There will not be any out-of-control right hooks. I am a lean, mean fighting machine, and all my punches are on the money." Missionary Scareaway began jumping around and throwing punches like Muhammad Ali. She told Mother Runnamouth, "You cannot be thinking you can handle me." Sister Backnibbler, with an attitude, said to Evangelist Trying, "We were told how you and the missionary were running your mouths about me and the elder. If you two have something to say about us, you need to be women enough to say it to our faces." The evangelist was shocked and said, "I have no idea what you are talking about, but if you are feeling froggy, you better find another pond to jump in. If you're thinking about jumping into this pond, you better think again, because you will not like the water." Sister Liketalie was agitated and asked, "What is wrong with everybody? Is everyone losing their minds? Can't you all see who is in the middle of all the mess?" Sister Aintwright walked over to Sister Liketalie, got in her face, and said to her, "You must think you are a seeing-eye profit. Do you have X-ray vision too?" Sister Liketalie did not back down. She asked Sister Aintwright, "Do you have a problem with me? If you do, we can solve it right now, right here."

Minister Wannado tried to calm everybody down. In his preacher voice, he told them, "This is not the way for church folk to act. 'Vengeance is mine saith the Lord.' YYou all need to let the Lord fight your battles." But no one listened, because they were at each other's throats. Mother Rongway just sat back and smiled at her work. In her sweet, loving, motherly voice, she said to Wannado, "I know you mean well, but they are beyond help. Let them go and just sit back with me and enjoy the show." At this point, everybody was arguing and fussing, not realizing that Mother Rongway was behind it all. She was truly an expert at starting mess. This went on for a while until Mother grew tired of them. She shouted loudly and got their attention. She told them, "You are all acting like a bunch of spoiled children." Minister Wannado tried to interrupt, but Mother told him to shut up. She said, "You have already said enough." She told them all, "I will not apologize, because I only told you all the truth the way I saw it. It is not my fault if you all took it the wrong way. Every one of you needs to get out of my house before I call the police and have you all arrested." Everyone stopped what they were doing and headed for the door to leave, because they knew Mother Rongway would stick to her word. They all left. Mother straightened up the room, went to her bedroom, and took a nap.

CHAPTER 6

MISSIONARY SCAREAWAY IS ENGAGED TO BE MARRIED

As time went on, all the members of the church would see one another at the grocery store or pass each other on the streets, sometimes speaking but sometimes not. Finally, they got over their differences and apologized to one another and stayed friends, or at least associates. They all had stopped going to church for a while but remained members of the Rongway First Liberation Church, mainly because there was no other parish to go to. Finally, they all decided to come back to church, and because of that, they were all still subject to whatever mess Mother Rongway cooked up.

Missionary Scareaway had been dating a guy for a little more than a year. They kept it a secret because they did not want anything or anyone to mess up their plans. He finally asked her to marry him, and of course she said yes. They then told everyone and set a date for their wedding. Everyone was happy for them, but of course Mother Rongway was a little upset that the missionary had not told her before she told everyone else. Missionary Scareaway and her husband-to-be did not want a long engagement to reduce the chances that someone could mess up their joyful day. Now that everyone knew, they could finally relax and plan their big day. Finally, the day came, and unbelievably, Mother Rongway insisted they have the wedding at her house.

It was another typical but beautiful morning in Rongway Peaks, and Mother Rongway was up early cleaning up her house because she had company stopping by soon. One of her girls, Missionary Scareaway, was getting married, and Mother Rongway was trying to get her house ready for the ceremony. But she was having second thoughts. So, as she straightened up the living room, she was fussing and talking to herself, wondering why she had insisted they have this wedding at her house. The more she thought about it, the angrier she got. Just then, the doorbell rang, and she shouted, wanting to know who it was; she was almost angry that someone was at her door. A voice from outside the door shouted back and said, "It is me, Mother Runnamouth, and the rest of the choir. We are here for rehearsal. Please hurry up and let us in. My feet are killing me."

Mother Rongway put a fake smile on her face and opened the door, and there stood Mother Runnamouth, Evangelist Trying, Deacon and Sister Aintwright, Brother and Sister Liketalie, and Deaconess Donothing. Mother Rongway quickly changed her bad disposition, put on her motherly charm, and told them, "Come on in." They all came in and spoke. Deaconess Donothing came in, and it was clear to see she was in a hurry. She asked Mother Rongway, "Can we go ahead and get started? I need to get back home as soon as possible and make myself beautiful for Missionary Scareaway's wedding. I know there will be some fine brothers at this wedding, and I plan to look so good that I will be engaged before it is over." Evangelist Trying laughed and agreed. She said, "I know that's right, and if Missionary Scareaway can get a husband, I know I can get myself one." She high-fived Deaconess Donothing. Sister Aintwright said, "I wasn't going to say anything, but the fact that Missionary Scareaway even got a husband is a miracle if you ask me." They all laughed. Sister Liketalie shouted in her high-pitched voice, and told them, "You all should not be talking about Missionary Scareaway like that, because she is our sister. We are here for rehearsal, not to talk about people." Brother Liketalie agreed and said, "My wife is right. We should not be talking about Missionary Scareaway like that." Then he asked Deacon Aintwright what he thought. Deacon Aintwright held up both hands and said, "I am just here for rehearsal. I am not getting into that. If Missionary Scareaway found somebody who was crazy enough" he paused, then said, "I meant *wise* enough to marry her, God bless her and him, poor guy."

Mother Rongway interrupted and told everybody, "That is enough about my girl. It is not Missionary Scareaway's fault that her mother kept dropping her on her head when she was a baby. We need to get started; I have a lot of cleaning and decorating to do." Then she asked Evangelist Trying, "Did you bring that new song you said you had? If so, let us hear it." Evangelist Trying got excited because she loved to sing. She told them, "It's a simple song, so everybody will be able to catch on without any problem." She started singing her song, "I Get Joy When I Think about the Food I Am About to Eat." They all began to sing. After they sang for a while, Mother Runnamouth had enough. She said, "That was a good warm-up, but we need to rehearse for real. We all got to get ready for Missionary Scareaway's wedding, and I plan to look good myself." Brother Liketalie jumped up and got excited. He agreed with Mother Runnamouth and said, "I got myself this bad outfit that is going to steal the show. I will be looking so good I know everybody will be thinking I am the one getting married."

That comment did not go over well with Sister Liketalie. She gave him an evil look and told him, "You are already married, remember? And to the finest woman in the Rongway First Liberation Church, if I say so myself. You need to cool it and not make me get ugly in Mother Rongway's house, because you know I can." Brother Liketalie, grinning, agreed and said, "Yes, dear, I am already married, and happily married at that. And you are so right, you are the finest woman in the Rongway First Liberation Church." Evangelist Trying, as she tried not to laugh, told everybody, "We better rehearse before things get ugly." The choir began to rehearse a real song. They really got into the song and tried to have some church for real. After a while, they all began to jump around and do their little dance. "Oh, glory!" shouted

Mother Rongway, almost out of breath. She said to them, "That was a real rehearsal, and the Rongway First Liberation Church choir still got it. Now I need everybody to get out so I can start decorating and cleaning up this house for the wedding."

They all said their goodbyes and left, except for Mother Runnamouth, who stayed to help Mother Rongway clean up and decorate for Missionary Scareaway's wedding. Mother Runnamouth sat down because she was tired and out of breath. She asked Mother Rongway, "Do you still need my help cleaning up and decorating? My feet are killing me." Mother Rongway laughed and told her, "If you stopped trying to squeeze them size ten feet into a size seven shoe, your feet would not hurt all the time, but that's just my personal opinion, and you don't have to take my word for it." Mother Runnamouth began to get upset. She asked Mother Rongway, "How can you open your crusty old lips and talk about my feet. Your feet are so big you can walk on water. Peter in the Bible does not have anything on you." Mother Rongway, in her loving, sweet, motherly voice, told Mother Runnamouth, "Do not get upset. I was just joking with you." Still upset, Mother Runnamouth stood up, put her hands on her hips, and began to move her head from side to side, saying, "That is fine and dandy. You may have been joking with me, but I was not joking with you. You really do have some big puppies."

This struck a nerve with Mother Rongway. She switched to a serious tone of voice. She said to Mother Runnamouth, "I was trying to be nice, but since you want to get stank, I may have big feet, but they are not even close to being as big as your mouth." Mother Runnamouth paced back and forth and shook her head. She called Mother by her first name, Rosalee, and said, "I came over here to help you because you said you needed my help getting your house ready for Missionary Scareaway's wedding, but I can leave. I do not need all this drama." Mother Rongway, once again in her loving, motherly voice told Mother Runnamouth, "I did not mean to upset you. We have been friends too long to be acting like this." She said she apologized, which she never did. Mother Runnamouth agreed and apologized also, feeling bad about the way she had acted. So, Mother Rongway suggested they get busy and get the house ready for her girl's wedding. They both began picking up stuff and started to decorate the house for the wedding.

As they began to work, they talked about Missionary Scareaway. Mother Rongway, as she hung some flowers on the wall, said, "I don't mean any harm, and Missionary Scareaway is one of my girls, but the missionary has a few issues." Mother Runnamouth stopped what she was doing, looked at Mother Rongway with a big smile on her face, and said, "I'm not one to start rumors, but since you brought it up, Missionary Scareaway does act a little strange sometimes." Then Mother Rongway asked her, "Have you seen that man the missionary is engaged to? I think I saw his twin brother at the zoo." They both laughed so hard they had to sit down. Mother Runnamouth agreed and said, "When Missionary Scareaway introduced me to him, the boy was so ugly I didn't know if I should speak or run." Now they were laughing so hard they were both in tears. They had stopped cleaning and decorating and were now just gossiping.

Mother Rongway, trying to compose herself, said, "I do not know how them two got together. I thought they had just met and barely knew one another, and the next thing I heard, they were engaged." Suddenly Mother Runnamouth stopped laughing and got upset and stood up. She said, "I do not see how Missionary Scareaway got so lucky. I have been looking for a husband for a long time now, and I cannot find one anywhere. Just look at me. I know I am still fine, and what man in his right mind would not want me?" Mother Rongway agreed and told her, "Go ahead and speak the truth. I know I am getting a little bit older, but I am like a fine wine: the older I get, the better I get." They high fived each other. Then Mother Rongway said, "I thought I did not want a husband, but since Deacon Rongway passed, I get so lonely sometimes. I know there is not a man anywhere who can resist a fine wine like me. I am vintage, and available." Mother Runnamouth stopped and said, "Wait a minute. You just said Deacon Rongway passed. Didn't you tell us he was out of town visiting his sister?" Mother, being quick on her feet, said, "Girl, do not pay any attention to me. This wedding has got me so stressed out I do not know what I am saying."

Mother Runnamouth sighed and said, "Whatever, but now I am depressed and do not feel good. This cleaning stuff is for the birds. You should have hired a housekeeper. This is too much work." Mother Rongway, laughing, asked her, "What do you think you are? The only difference is I do not have to pay you, and I would have to pay a housekeeper. You come cheap." Mother Runnamouth did not like that and said, "I don't see anything funny." She sat back down, put her feet up, and said, "I think I will just sit here for a while and take a break. Since I am cheap help, then I will give cheap labor." Mother Rongway replied, with a slight smile on her face, and told Mother Runnamouth, "Do not get upset again. You should know we are homegirls. Come on and help me get this house ready for the wedding. I cannot do it without your help. I need you." Mother Runnamouth complained and said, "I do not see why I should be the one to help clean up and decorate in the first place. It is not my wedding. Missionary Scareaway should be the one helping you. Why didn't you ask her to help?"

Mother Rongway laughed and said to Mother Runnamouth, "You must be kidding. Remember, we both have been in Missionary Scareaway's house and know that cleaning is not exactly her anointing." They both laughed. Mother Runnamouth, still laughing, said, "Unless her new husband is a pig and doesn't mind living in a pigpen, or at least know how to clean a pigpen, he is in trouble." Mother Rongway agreed but just could not miss an opportunity to stir up more mess. She asked Mother Runnamouth, "Didn't your first husband leave you because you could not cook, and your house was so nasty he had to use a navigation system to get from one room to the next? That is just what I heard, but I could be wrong." Mother Runnamouth stood up, and now she was more than upset, she was angry. She told Mother Rongway, "Hold up and stop the music. Somebody needs to call Pastor Whocares, because I am about to perform a miracle. I am about to put my fist in your mouth and pull out all your teeth at the same time, which will not be too hard since they are false."

Mother Rongway told her, "Wait one cotton-picking minute. I know I am a little older than you are, but since I got you here at my house to help me clean up, I will use you like a rag mop to mop up the floor. Do not make me get ugly, because you know I can." Mother Runnamouth got into her so-called karate stance and shouted back and reminded Mother Rongway that she knew karate. She said, "My hands are lethal weapons, so come on and bring it, Mother-zilla," referring to God-zilla. Mother Rongway walked over to the table, picked up her pocketbook, and said to her, "Come on, Bruce Runnamouth," referring to Bruce Lee. Then she told Mother Runnamouth, "You must have forgotten that I have a switchblade. Do not make me bring Little Willie out of retirement. If I do, one of us will have to be carried out of this house on a stretcher, and it will not be me."

At that point Mother Runnamouth was in full-blown fight mode. She cried out "Oh, junk!" as she tied a band around her head and got into her karate stance. She told Mother Rongway, "You done it now. I was just planning to teach you a lesson, but you need a good, old-fashioned whipping. Come on and show me what you are working with." Mother Rongway switched back to her soft, calm voice and told Mother Runnamouth, "You need to calm down. You know I gave up cutting people a long time ago when I caught religion, but you are about to make me lose my religion, and I had a tough time catching it. Now that I caught it, do not make me lose it again." Mother Runnamouth, sarcastically, said to Mother Rongway, "I do not know where you caught your religion at, but evidently you caught the wrong one. The one you say you caught is not really working. You are still that same mean old woman you were twenty years ago. You have not changed one bit. I suggest you go somewhere and try to catch another religion."

Mother Rongway looked at Mother Runnamouth, shook her head, and spoke in such a loving, motherly voice. She told her, "Since I am a changed woman, I am trying my best to leave Little Willie in retirement, but you just keep asking for it. Normally when someone keeps asking me for something, I try my best to give them what they are asking for if I can. I do not understand why you keep asking me to cut you. If you keep insisting, I will not have no other choice." Now this really got Mother Runnamouth going. She grunted and snarled as she asked Mother Rongway, "Are you really going to cut me? I guess you are a crazy old church mother with a switchblade knife. How many states are you wanted in? I know the police have to be looking for you right now. I wonder how much reward money I can get for turning you in?"

As you can imagine, that did not sit too well with Mother Rongway, especially the part about the police, so she tried to make things right. She used her sweet, motherly voice again and told Mother Runnamouth to hold up. She said to her, "We have known each other too long for us to be acting like this. We need to just calm down and stop acting like a couple of teenagers." Mother Runnamouth, still upset, did not feel the same way. She told Mother Rongway, "I am not acting. You made me mad, and the only thing that is going to satisfy me now is to whip your back end. Neither your sweet talk nor anything else will change my mind, so you can come on and take your whipping like a woman." Mother Rongway walked over to where Mother Runnamouth was standing and put her arm around her shoulder, trying to calm her down. She pled with her and told her, "You should know you are my homegirl. We have been best friends for as long as I can remember. We should stop all this foolishness and get this house cleaned up and decorated."

Mother Runnamouth sat down, still upset, and said, "I do not know if I want to be your homegirl right now, and I am certainly not in the mood to clean anymore. I need to go home and take a nap because I am tired." Suddenly Mother Rongway perked up and said, "I have just the thing guaranteed to change our mood. I have some special music that I know will make us both feel better." She walked over to her CD player and put on her special music—certainly not the kind of music you would expect the church mother to have. As soon as Mother Runnamouth heard the music, she forgot everything that had just transpired. Her mood changed; she put a smile on her face and forgot she said she was tired. She jumped up and began to breakdance to the music. She shouted to Mother Rongway and said, "Come on and show me what you can do." Mother Rongway, who was now also dancing, began to do the running man, the tootsie roll, and the robot. The two of them were doing dances from back in the day that no one does anymore. Mother Rongway, now in her rhythm, told Mother Runnamouth, in a very high-pitched voice, "We still got it!" And then she screamed to Mother Runnamouth, "Work it, girl, work it!"

Mother Runnamouth yelled back, because the music was so loud, "I thought we were getting old, but we are not getting old, just getting better. The young folk do not have anything on us." She yelled to Mother Rongway, "Go on and get down with the get-down" They both began to shake it to the east and shake it to the west, forgetting all about what they were supposed to be doing. This went on for a while until the doorbell rang. It was Mother Rongway's granddaughter, Toddie Rongway, who had been out of town for a couple of weeks. Outside the door, Toddie screamed loudly, trying to be heard over the music. She yelled to her grandmother to open the door. She said, "I know someone is in there because I can hear the music playing. Do not make me break down this door, because I will if I must." Mother Rongway stopped dancing and hurried to change the music in a real panic. She yelled and told Mother Runnamouth, "We got caught. There is somebody at the door, and I think it is my granddaughter Toddie." She yelled and told Mother Runnamouth, "Get the door while I change the CD." Mother Runnamouth was so caught up in the music and her dancing that she did not hear Mother Rongway calling to her.

CHAPTER 7

Toddie and The Scareaway's Have a Face Off

Meanwhile outside the door, Toddie was getting upset. Toddie screamed as loud as she could and asked her grandmother, "Are you going to open this door or what? It is hot out here, and if I get a sunstroke, Grandmother, you will be sorry." Mother Rongway yelled back and told her, "Just a minute, I'm coming," as she scrambled to find a gospel CD. She looked over at Mother Runnamouth, who was still dancing, and screamed at her once again. She asked her, "Are you deaf or something?" She told her once again, "Go to the door. I think it is my granddaughter, Toddie." Finally, Mother Runnamouth realized that the music was no longer playing and stopped dancing. She said to Mother Rongway, "My bad, but I was in another time zone for a minute and did not hear you. That music took me back to when I was in my prime. I could dance all night." Mother Runnamouth asked Mother Rongway, "What did you say?" Mother Rongway told her, "I said get the door. I think it's my granddaughter, Toddie."

They both got spiritual. Mother Runnamouth went to the door, making sure her hair and clothes were in place. She opened the door and told Toddie to come on in. Toddie asked, "What took you so long to open the door? You both know I am sensitive and cannot stay outside too long. Me and the sun do not get along. You two old people would have felt bad if I would have had a sunstroke." Mother Rongway walked over to where Toddie was standing and put her arm around her to comfort her. She told her, "I am sorry, and I did not mean to leave you out there like that. Please do not be upset with your ole grandmother. You are too pretty to be upset." She turned to Mother Runnamouth and asked, "Isn't that right?" At that moment, Mother Runnamouth grabbed her pocketbook, took out a candy bar, and took a big bite. She turned her back on them both and began to chew as fast as she could so she would not have to respond to Mother Rongway's question. Toddie looked at her in disgust and told her, "You are not funny." Then she turned her attention back to Mother Rongway. She said to her grandmother, "That music that is now playing is not the same music I heard when I was knocking on your door. What I heard was not gospel music, so do not even try to fool me."

Mother Rongway, in her soft, motherly voice, called her *baby* as she walked back over to the CD player and turned it off. Then she told Toddie, "You know your ole grandmother does not play but one kind of music in my house. This house is a holy house." Then she shouted, "Oh, glory!" She threw up both hands and waved them in the air, then said, "I do not even allow that mess in my house. You should know that." Mother Runnamouth agreed and told Toddie, "You should also know I do not listen to but one kind of music, and that is gospel music. I am a holy woman and only listen to holy music." Toddie began to move her head from side to side and said, "I know you two call yourselves holy mothers, but the music I heard did not have anything to do with being holy. I bet the two of you were in here trying to get down." Mother Rongway told her, "Not only am I your grandmother, but I'm Mother Rongway, mother of the Rongway First Liberation Church, and when I tell you something, it isn't anything but the truth." And she asked Mother Runnamouth to agree.

Mother Runnamouth hesitated for a moment as she looked back in her mind. She told Mother Rongway, "I do seem to remember a few times you bent, twisted, stretched, misquoted, or left out part of the truth, or maybe you just forgot what the truth was." Mother Rongway looked at her, snarled, and said, "I never said that I was perfect. I may have gotten confused a couple of times, but that is all it was: confusion. I do not lie." Toddie got loud and said, "I don't care if you two stand on your heads and spin like a top." Then she paused and said, "That would impress me, but right now, I'm hungry." She asked her grandmother if she would fix her something to eat. Mother Runnamouth sarcastically said to Toddie, "I don't mean any harm, but you look like it would not hurt you to skip a few meals, but that's just my opinion, and you do not have to take my word for it."

That struck a nerve. Toddie screamed and said, "I am not fat, I am just fluffy! And if you cannot see that, then something is wrong with your eyes. You need to go to the eye doctor and get your eyes checked." Toddie walked over to the couch, slammed herself down in the seat, and started crying. Mother Rongway went over and sat beside Toddie and tried to comfort her. She called her *baby* and told her, "There is no need to cry. Of course, you are not fat; you just have big bones like your grandmother. People think I am fat too, but I just have big bones." Mother Runnamouth started laughing. She told them, "If you two have big bones, I hope they do not get any bigger, or you both can get a job in the Thanksgiving Day Parade as one of those humongous floating balloons."

At that point, Toddie really began to cry. Toddie was not Mother Rongway's real granddaughter. Her parents were drug addicts and had abandoned Toddie when she was a baby. Mother Rongway adopted her, and because Mother was so old when she got Toddie, she raised Toddie as her granddaughter. Toddie never knew who her birth parents were, and Mother Rongway never told her. She grew up seeing all the crooked, mean, and devious stuff that Mother Rongway did. She grew up following in Mother Rongway's footsteps. She looked up to her grandmother and thought she could do no wrong. She was taught by the best at what she did. Mother Rongway looked at Mother Runnamouth, rolled her eyes, and told her, "Look at what you have done." She tried to comfort Toddie and told her, "Do not mind Mother

Runnamouth, because she has issues. Stop crying, and we will go to the store and get something to cook." She looked at Mother Runnamouth and told her, "Come on, Mother Run Your Mouth!"

Mother Runnamouth put her hands on her hips, moved her neck from side to side, and said to Mother Rongway, "Excuse me. I always heard that if you tell the truth, you will shame the devil. If people cannot stand the truth, they need to stay out the kitchen." Then, unexpectedly, Mother Runnamouth began to sing an old song titled "If You Cannot Stand the Grease, You Need to Stay out the Kitchen." Meanwhile, Mother Rongway got up, got her pocketbook, and headed toward the door. She told Mother Runnamouth, once again, "Come on if you can stop singing long enough. We should leave before you upset my baby again." And they both left.

Toddie stopped crying and got herself together. She said, "I thought those two old birds would never leave." Then she got up and began to look for the music her grandmother had been playing. She found the CD, put the music back on, started dancing and shouted, "Go, Grandmother! Go, Grandmother! It's your birthday, it's your birthday!" Toddie turned the music off and sat back down. She took a minute to calm down and decided to call who she said was her future husband. She said to herself, "I know he is sitting by the phone waiting for me to call." She picked up the phone and dialed the number. A voice on the other end said hello, and she said, "Hey, baby, it's me." The voice on the phone said, "Who is this?" She paused, then shouted, "What do you mean 'Who is this?' It is your future wife, that is who!" The voice on the phone called her someone else. That really got her upset. By now she was almost screaming and told him, "No, this is not Sister Knowsall. I would not want to be that skinny if someone paid me. This is not a crank call, and it is not April Fools' Day either. You should know it is me, Toddie, Mother Rongway's granddaughter."

Suddenly she heard a click, and the line went dead. Toddie was now fuming. She said, "I know my future husband did not just hang up on me. Something must have happened to the phone." She dialed his number again, and in a sweet, calm voice, she said, "Hello, Minister Wannado, honey. I know you did not just hang up on me." She heard another click; he had hung up again. Toddie screamed again and said, "Just wait until I get my hands on that Minister Wannado. He does not realize who he is messing with. My grandmother is Rosalee Rongway." At that moment, the doorbell rang, and Toddie screamed really loudly, asking who was at the door. A voice from outside the door shouted back and said, "It is Missionary Scareaway and my auntie Gertrude from down South. Can we come in?" Toddie mumbled under her breath and said, "This is just what I need, the prayer cap crusaders. Anointed Woman and her sidekick, Holy Ghost Junior."

She got up, opened the door, and told them, "Come on in, but my grandmother and Mother Runnamouth are not here. They will be right back. They had to go to the store for a quick minute." Missionary Scareaway spoke with excitement in her voice. She said to Toddie, "I have not seen you in a month of Sundays. You remember my aunt, Evangelist Scareaway. That is where I get my good looks. I look just like my favorite aunt." Toddie began to laugh uncontrollably as Missionary Scareaway and Evangelist Scareaway looked at her, wondering what she found so funny. Toddie, trying to control herself, said, "I thought Missionary Scareaway was making a joke, because that was funny. I needed a good laugh, and that was right on time." Evangelist Scareaway snarled and spoke, telling Toddie, "I can see you still need Jesus. People can talk about me as much as they please. The more they talk, I will break their knees." The missionary tried to correct her and said, "That is not exactly how that saying goes. It says the more you talk, I will bend my knees, or something like that."

Evangelist Scareaway looked at her with an expression on her face that said that was *her* version. She told her, "You can bend your knees if you want to, but I am not that saved yet. I have only been saved ten years." Toddie started laughing again and said to her, "You got to be kidding. You just told me that I need Jesus. You need a complete transfiguration or something. It sounds like you got a few issues of your own, but you do not have to take my word for it; just ask your shrink." Missionary Scareaway tried to make an excuse for her aunt's behavior. She told Toddie, "Do not pay my aunt any attention. She had a rough childhood, but do not talk about her like that. We just came by to see how the wedding preparations are coming along and if Mother Rongway needs any help." Evangelist Scareaway looked around the room, turned up her nose, and asked the missionary, "Do you really want to have your wedding in this house? If so, you got to be out of your mind. This house is a disaster. It needs a lot of work." Toddie got upset and told her to wait just a minute. She told her, "Do not be talking about my grandmother's house. I will tell her what you said, and you know she will punch you in your face. So, I advise you to zip your lips."

Evangelist Doris Scareaway came from a very dysfunctional home. Her mother and father stayed together, but they fussed and fought all the time. They never showed her or her sisters any kind of love. She grew up cold, not caring about anyone but herself. She always said what was on her mind, no matter who it offended. She never got married but did have a son at an incredibly early age. Her oldest sister, who was Missionary Scareaway's mother, died a few years after having the missionary. The evangelist took the missionary in and raised her until her eighteenth birthday. Not knowing how to show her love, she told her it was time for her to move out and make a life for herself. The missionary did and ended up in Rongway Peaks. She joined the Rongway First Liberation Church, and Mother Rongway made her a missionary.

Once again, Missionary Scareaway tried to make excuses for her aunt. She told Toddie, "My Aunt Gertrude does not mean any harm. You know she has a sharp tongue, and sometimes she has a quick tongue." Evangelist Scareaway said, "There is not anything wrong with my tongue, and there is not anything wrong with my eyes either. You need to have your wedding somewhere else. I would not want you to have your wedding here if this were the last house on earth." Toddie agreed and told the missionary, "Your aunt is such a wise woman, and you should listen to her. I too think you should have your wedding somewhere else." At that moment, the doorbell rang. Toddie yelled out as loudly as she could asking who was at the door. A loud voice outside the door replied and said, "It is June Bug Scareaway. Will somebody please open this door and let me in? I have been driving all day, and I am tired."

Toddie shook her head in disbelief and start talking to herself again, but this time, other people were around to hear what she was saying. She said, "I do not believe this, and where is my grandmother when I need her? We are being invaded by aliens, and she is not home. I cannot manage all these little green people by myself." She walked over and opened the door. June Bug came in, but before he could speak, chaos erupted again. Missionary Scareaway, now upset, told Toddie to hold up and wait one minute. She said to her, "I know you did not just call us aliens. Somebody please tell me that is not what I heard Toddie say." Evangelist Scareaway yelled, "Yes, she did, and I heard her with my own two ears. I will not take being called names from this disrespectful heathen. I will body-slam her in her grandmother's house." Brother June Bug shouted at his mother and asked, "What is going on in this house? What have you and my cousin gotten into now? It seems to me that everywhere you go, you start trouble." Toddie broke into their conversation and said, "I do not know if anybody noticed or not, but I am not as tiny as I may look, so you, Miss Evangelist, might want to rethink that whole body-slamming idea. That really is not an option, so you might want to try and come up with something else."

Laughing, Missionary Scareaway agreed. She went on to say, "Jumbo the whale doesn't have anything on you." They all began to laugh, but Toddie did not see anything funny. Toddie got terribly upset and began to pace around the room. She told them they had done it now. She said, "I am about to flip out and whip everybody up in here. I am Mother Rongway's granddaughter, and you all know she does not take any junk, and neither do I. If everybody knows what is best, you all might want to leave while you can still walk." Just as Toddie finished her statement, Mother Rongway opened the door. She and

Mother Runnamouth were finally back from the store. They came in with their bags, and Mother Rongway called for Toddie. She said, "We are back." She saw Evangelist Scareaway and Brother June Bug along with Missionary Scareaway standing in the living room. Sarcastically, Mother Rongway said, "Bless my soul and fry me a jackrabbit; look who is here. It is the sanctified hillbillies and Missionary Scareaway."

Mother Runnamouth, surprised to see them, said, "It is Evangelist Gertrude and Brother June Bug. How are you two doing? You two look like new money fresh off the counterfeit machine." Evangelist Scareaway turned her head and turned up her nose, and said, "It is Mother Runnamouth. I have not seen you in years. I see you are still wearing them same broke-down old wigs, and you look like you slept in the one you have on now." Toddie walked over to where Evangelist Scareaway was standing and told her, "I know you are old, but I am not afraid to beat up on old people. I will knock those false teeth right out of your mouth." Mother Rongway told Toddie, "Calm down and do not worry your pretty self about Evangelist Scareaway. The Good Book does say that her tongue is the root of all her evil."

Mother Runnamouth gave Evangelist Scareaway an evil look, because she was upset and ready to fight again. She told the evangelist, "I do not care what Mother Rongway or the Good Book say. You have insulted me, and vengeance is mine. Come on, Evangelist Scareaway. I am about to baptize you in the middle of this floor." Missionary Scareaway screamed for everybody to hold up and stop all that drama. She asked, "Why can't you all just get along? This is my wedding, and I want it to be special, but the way things are going, it is turning into a circus." Brother June Bug agreed. He asked his Mother, "What is wrong with you and everyone else in this house? I thought we came over to Mother Rongway's house to see if there is anything we can do to help, not start a fight." Evangelist Scareaway tried to defend her position. She said, "That is exactly why we came over here, but you know Mother Rongway has always plucked my last nerve; but for my pretty niece and her big day, I will try to endure this hardness as a good soldier. I am a godly woman." Mother Rongway began to laugh and said, "Yeah, right. The soldier part I agree with, and I bet I can guess whose army you belong to. He has two horns and a long tail, and he is red."

Mother Runnamouth, laughing, could not wait to add in her unwanted opinion. She told Mother Rongway, "I know that it is a fact that Evangelist Scareaway got kicked out of the devil's army. The two of them could not get along because the evangelist tried to take over and run it her way." At that point, Brother June Bug spoke up. He told them that was enough. He said, "You all have talked enough junk about my mother. I will be the first to admit she is not perfect, and yes, she may need to see a head doctor, but she is still my mother, and nobody wants me to go off up in here." Toddie cleared her throat and walked over to where Brother June Bug was standing. In a stern, loud voice, she told him, "Do not make me laugh. I will sit on you and squash you like the June bug you are."

Brother June Bug was an only child. He never had any friends because his mother was not very sociable, so he always stayed to himself. He was small in stature and never learned how to fight. When Missionary Scareaway came to live with them, they bonded and began to look out for one another. The missionary had to fight many times defending his honor. His mouth always got him into trouble. He tried to be the head of the household, but fear always took over. When Missionary Scareaway moved out, June Bug stayed at home with his mother, since he never got married and still lived with his mother. Now he was in a situation where his maturity would be tested.

Brother June Bug became upset and tried to get tough, telling Toddie, "Come on, sumo wrestler. I am not scared of you." Although she was twice his size, he told her he would take her on. But fear took over, and he got behind his mother, Evangelist Scareaway. Missionary Scareaway started crying and sat down on the couch, hard. She told them, "You all are going to mess up my wedding. I thought this was supposed to be about me. I am the one getting married. Can you all act like sensible people for once?" Evangelist Scareaway tried to comfort her and said, "I am sorry. You are right. It is your day." She looked at Mother Rongway and attempted to speak in a civil tone of voice, asking her, "Can we try and get along for the sake of this wedding, and can you please control your watchdog before I call the dog pound?" Mother Rongway said, "I do not have a problem myself, because I am a godly woman. Missionary Scareaway is one of my girls." She looked at her granddaughter, Toddie, and told her to calm down. She told her, "Just plead the blood on these demons, and you will be fine. That is what I do."

Mother Runnamouth agreed and said, "Mother Rongway is right. Missionary Scareaway is our girl, and we should all try and get along for her wedding." She turned around, looked at Evangelist Scareaway, and told her, "As soon as the wedding is over, it is the two of us outside. We have some unfinished business to take care of." Evangelist Scareaway agreed and told her, "For once in your life, you are right, and I know the Lord is going to give me the strength to knock you out. The Good Book does say He will give me the strength to fight my enemies." Brother June Bug interrupted and tried to calm everyone down. He said, "Everybody needs to take it easy. We all are tired, and maybe a little stressed out because of this wedding. That is no reason to ruin my cousin's big day. We all need to put aside our feelings and let this be about Missionary Scareaway." Toddie, still ready to fight, told him, "A few minutes ago you was ready to go off, so do not try to act like Mister Goody-Two-Shoes now. I will still come over there and punch you in the face. Wedding or no wedding, it does not make any difference to me."

Missionary Scareaway began to cry very loudly. She said, "I think me and Brother Moanback need to elope. Everybody in this house has some serious issues. My wedding is going to be a disaster." Mother Rongway comforted her and reassured her that everything would be all right. She told her, "Do not get upset, because Mother's got this. I want everybody to leave my house right now so I can get it ready for my girl's wedding. I would hate—"Then she paused, changed her statement, and spoke in such a loving voice, saying, "I mean, it will hurt me to my heart to have to cut somebody." Evangelist Scareaway, with an attitude, told June Bug and Missionary Scareaway, "It's time for us to get out of this broke-down old house because them two old crows have to be on crack." She told Mother Rongway, "You have not changed a bit. You still need Jesus." They all got up and headed for the door. Mother Runnamouth pleaded with Mother Rongway and said to her, "Please let me hit the evangelist just one time with my two lethal weapons," as she held up both hands. She said, "I promise we will not have any more problems out of her." Mother Rongway told Mother Runnamouth, "I am sure you think your hands are lethal weapons but let her go. We both know she is demon-possessed and the only thing that will help her is an exorcism." Mother Runnamouth began to laugh and agreed. She said, "I was waiting for her head to start spinning around and lightning to shoot out of her eyes."

CHAPTER 8

THE LIKETALIES TRIED TO STAND UP TO MOTHER RONGWAY

In the meantime, Toddie sat down and began looking through a book that was lying on the table. She said, "I know that is right. That June Bug was getting on my reserve nerve. A few more minutes, and I was about to body-slam him in the middle of the floor." Mother Rongway said, "They have all left, and we will not have to see them again until the wedding. I am going in the kitchen and fix my Toddie a snack." She asked Mother Runnamouth to give her a hand in the kitchen and started to leave the room. Sarcastically Mother Runnamouth said, "Sure, because I do not have a life. I am just here to serve Mother Rongway. Whatever you say, Mother. Whatever you want, Mother. Whatever you need, Mother. That is my whole mission in life." Mother Rongway stopped abruptly, turned around, and looked at Mother Runnamouth. She asked her, "What is wrong with you? You need to stop all the drama and give me a hand in the kitchen, seeing as I asked you so nicely."

Finally, they left and went to the kitchen. Toddie felt relieved and said, "Those two need to lay off those old people drugs they been taking. I do not know what it is, but it is starting to scramble their brains." She said to herself, "Now that I am alone, I need to call my future husband again and see what he is doing." She took out her cellphone and dialed his number. A voice on the other end said hello. In the sexiest, most romantic voice she could find, Toddie said, "Hello Minister Wannado. It is me, your future wife. We got cut off the last time we spoke, and I know it was no fault of yours." Suddenly Toddie heard the dial tone again. The minister had hung up the phone. Toddie shouted, "No he did not!" Now she was furious. She said, "I know he did not just hang up on me again." She said to herself, "Just wait until I get my hands on that Minister Wannado." She stopped and realized what she had just said. A big smile came on her face, then she said to herself again, "Wait until I get my hands all over that Minister Wannado." Just at that moment, the doorbell rang again. Angry at being interrupted in the middle of her fantasy, she screamed very loudly, "Who is it?" A voice on the other side of the door shouted back loudly and said, "It is Brother and Sister Liketalie. We are here for Missionary Scareaway's wedding. Can we come in?" Toddie sighed and said aloud, "Here we go again," and she got up to go to the door. She said to herself, "Some more of them crazy church folk. I do not see how my grandmother does it. All the members at her church have some serious issues."

She opened the door. Toddie told them, "Come on in. My grandmother will be out shortly. She and Mother Runnamouth are in the kitchen." She told them to have a seat and relax their feet. They came in and began to talk. Sister Liketalie laughed and told Toddie, "I have not seen you since you was a little girl, but you sure are not little anymore. In fact—" She paused to find the right words, then said, "You are very healthy." Brother Liketalie began laughing so hard he could barely control himself. He told his wife, "You can call it that if you want to, but I think little Toddie done turned into big Toddie or large Toddie or humongous Toddie, but that is just my observation." Toddie glared at him with an evil look and said, "Okay, I get the point," and called him Bubba the Clown. She said, "Personally, I do not see anything funny other than the way you look. Now that is funny." Sister Liketalie, trying not to laugh, told Bubba, "You need to stop. Toddie is not really that large; she is just pleasantly plump, that is all."

Brother Liketalie walked over to the couch and sat down, still laughing. He told her, "Okay, whatever you say, but you know you need to get your eyes checked. If you cannot see how huge Toddie done got, I think you need glasses, and bad." Toddie got upset and spoke out of anger. She told them, "I think I will go to my room before I hurt Bubba the Clown, and I am too pretty to be acting like that. I need to go and cool off." She left the room. Sister Liketalie, now upset with Bubba, told him, "You done it again. You hurt Toddie's feelings. No matter where we go, every time you open your mouth, you put your big foot in it." Brother Liketalie told Johnnie Sue, "Wait one minute, because you know that is not true. First of all, my feet are not that big, and second of all, your feet are much bigger than mine, and you know I cannot put my foot in my mouth. My mouth will not open that wide." Sister Liketalie said, "Whatever," and she sat down beside him. She told him, "I do not want to argue with you. This is supposed to be a happy day, so we do not need to mess it up for Missionary Scareaway."

Brother Liketalie leaned back on the couch and expressed his inner thoughts aloud. He said, "Missionary Scareaway is getting married. If I were not invited to the wedding, I would not believe it. She is nice and all, but sister girl has a few issues going on. I do not think anybody could have seen marriage in her future." Sister Liketalie, laughing, said, "I did not want to say anything, because I thought I was the only one who noticed. The missionary does seem to have a few problems. I never dreamed she would be getting married." Bubba said, "Thank God we do not have to worry about her problems. Her new husband-to-be will have his hands full. Poor Brother Moanback. I hope he knows what he is getting himself into." Sister Liketalie agreed and said, "If you ask me, he isn't playing with a full deck either." She asked Bubba if he had seen Brother Moanback. Brother Liketalie scratched his head, trying to remember. Then he told her, "No, I do not think I have seen him, but I hear he is something else. Somebody told me he is a good-looking guy." He asked her if she had seen him. She told him, "Yes, I have. He is good-looking, all right. He looks like a bullfrog on crack, if you ask me. I know Missionary Scareaway may have a few issues, but even she could have done better than that. I would not wish that on my worst enemy. The missionary must be desperate."

Brother Liketalie, also laughing, said, "Maybe she is, but like I said, that is not our problem. Missionary Scareaway is the one who has to look at him every morning when she wakes up; we do not." Sister Liketalie, with a sigh of relief, said, "Thank God for that. It is hard enough to wake up every morning and look at you. I am glad I do not have to wake up and look at another woman's ugly husband too." Brother Liketalie looked at her in awe. He told her, "Now you got jokes. You did not say that ten years ago when you begged me to marry you. As I recall, you said I was the best-looking man who had ever asked you out, and I happen to agree. I know I look good, so I know you are not talking about me." Sister Liketalie looked at him and told him, "Do not make me laugh, and do not flatter yourself. The only reason I married you is because your father paid me to. Your father told me that was the only way to get you out of his house. There you was, a grown man, and still living at home with your mommy and daddy like a little boy."

Brother Liketalie began to laugh and said, "Does that not beat all. Your mother paid me to marry you. Your mother said she had to get rid of you because you was eating them out of house and home, and I know the feeling. You eat so much you must have a twin. There is no way one person can eat as much as you do." At that statement, he got up and moved out of the way quickly, expecting her to throw a punch. Sister Liketalie stood to her feet, visibly upset, and asked him, "What are you trying to say, and why did you move way to the other side of the room? Since you so bad, come closer and say that." She paused. Then she told him, "I am waiting, and what do you have to say to that?" Brother Liketalie, now cowardly standing on the other side of the room, said to her, "No, thank you, I am fine right where I am. You need to calm down. You should not be acting like this in somebody else's house, especially Mother Rongway's house. That woman will come in here and throw the both of us out on our heads."

Sister Liketalie went off, not realizing that Mother Rongway was now standing in the doorway. She got loud, "I am not scared of Mother Rongway. If she messes with me, I will slap the taste out of her mouth. If that is not enough, I will knock that wig off her old bald head." Bubba tried to let her know that Mother Rongway was standing behind her, but it was too late. Once Sister Liketalie realized what Bubba was trying to tell her, she slowly turned around and saw Mother Rongway standing there, then she fainted. Brother Liketalie rushed over to where she fell, knelt, and tried to revive her. He shouted and asked her, "Are you all right? Speak to me. What is wrong with you? Get up, because you are getting your clothes dirty, and I just washed them yesterday." Mother Rongway told him to leave her alone while looking in the other direction, deliberately not looking at Sister Liketalie. She said to him, "Let her stay down there while I calm down. The Lord works in mysterious ways."

She raised both her hands. She said, "Since I caught religion, the Lord knows I am trying to be good, so He knocked Sister Liketalie out so I would not have to. Just let her stay down there and repent so the church can roll on." Brother Liketalie tried to get some courage to stand up to Mother Rongway. He stood up and left Johnnie Sue lying there. He told Mother, "I am not what people would call a religious man, and I did not catch religion like you said you did, which I do not believe, so I will give you a piece of my mind." Mother Rongway began to laugh. She told him, "You need to be careful, because you know you only have half a mind. If you start giving that away, you might short-circuit. You are functioning with only one or two brain cells already."

Brother Liketalie told her she was funny. He went on to say, "Since we are talking, I think you are a backbiting, two-faced, hypocritical, lying old woman. I have never even heard of anybody like you." Mother Rongway was amazed by him and his boldness. She told him he needed help. She said to him, "You have a demon in you, and I think you need an exorcism. Come over here where I am standing and let me cast that demon out, or at least beat him out. That demon done took complete control of your tongue, because I know you do not have the nerve to talk to me like that unless you have a death wish." Just then Sister Liketalie opened her eyes and got up off the floor. She called her husband in a very shallow voice and asked, "What happened, and why are you standing all the way over there? What is going on, and why are you sweating as if it were a hundred degrees in here?" Brother Liketalie, almost in tears, told her, "I think we need to get out of this house. It is not safe in here. That woman is crazy." He pointed at Mother Rongway. He said, "We need to leave before somebody has to carry us out on a stretcher."

Mother Rongway then walked over to Brother Liketalie, put her arm around his neck, and spoke very softly. She called him *baby* and told him, "You need to come over and sit down. You look as if you are about to pass out. Can I get you something to drink?" She agreed with his wife that he was sweating like a waterfall. Once again Sister Liketalie asked him, "What is wrong with you? You are shaking like a leaf on a tree, and you look like you have seen the devil himself." Brother Liketalie, in a low, sniffling voice told her, "I did not see the devil with the horns and the long tail, but I do know the devil's sister when I see her, and she is standing right over there." He pointed at Mother Rongway again. He told Sister Liketalie, "We need to get out of this house right now." Sister Liketalie told him, "You can leave if you want to, but I came over here for Missionary Scareaway's wedding, and I am not leaving until it is over." She walked over to the couch and sat down.

Mother Rongway began to laugh. She told Sister Liketalie, "Either you have a lot of nerve or you are as dumb as a tree stump. If I were in your shoes and said all that stuff you just said about me, I would be running." Mother Rongway saw an opportunity to mess with them, so she made up a lie. She told them, "Unless you two are planning to spend the night, and my house is not a Motel 6, so I don't leave the light on for anybody, you two brave souls are a little early for Missionary Scareaway's wedding." She lied and said it was not until the next day, in the afternoon. Brother Liketalie, extremely upset, said to Johnnie Sue,

"You dragged me over here to this demonic house to be attacked by this, this . . ." Mother Rongway stopped him before he could finish his statement. She told him, "Hold your horses, Mr. Motormouth. I do not know if you just lost your memory and do not remember whose house you are in, or if you are just as dumb as your wife. Unless you want to take your teeth home in a paper bag, I suggest you study to be quiet."

Sister Liketalie jumped up off the couch. Now she was upset. She told Bubba, "Come on, and let's go," almost screaming. She told him, "You are so right about this house being demon-possessed. Just being in this house makes me want to lose my religion and slap somebody, and you know I am not afraid to hit an old woman. Remember I said earlier that I would knock that wig right off her bald head? So let us go." Then she got behind Bubba as they walked backward slowly towards the door. Mother Rongway laughed and mocked Sister Liketalie. She said to her, "I did not know you were a comedian. You have jokes. You do not have any religion, but you do have jokes. I did not know the two of you were so wise. I have to say, that is smart. Backing out the door and not turning your backs to me is the smartest thing you two have done all day." They both backed out the door very slowly and ran to their car.

CHAPTER 9
T<small>ODDIE</small>'<small>S</small> E<small>NCOUNTER WITH THE</small> B<small>ACKNIBBLERS</small>

Just then Toddie entered from the bedroom, where she had been taking a nap. She yelled and asked her grandmother what all that noise was. She said, "I was trying to get my beauty rest, and somebody woke me up. You know I need my beauty sleep." Mother Rongway apologetically told Toddie, "I am so sorry, and we did not mean to wake you. I really forgot you were in the house, but since you are up, you can help straighten up the living room. Them Liketalies made a mess in my house. I must go out for a while, and I will be back later." Toddie said to her, "Wait a minute, and where are you going? Why should I have to clean up? I did not make the mess. Why didn't you make them Liketalies clean up since they were the ones who made the mess in the first place?" Mother Rongway told her, "Just cleanup for me and stop complaining. Since you need to know everything I do, me and Mother Runnamouth have to go to the store to get some more stuff for Missionary Scareaway's wedding."

She then called out to Mother Runnamouth, who was still in the kitchen, and asked her if she was coming with her. Toddie looked at her grandmother saying, "We need to sit down and have a discussion. I thought my wedding was supposed to be the first wedding in your house. What happened to that?" At that moment, Mother Runnamouth came into the room and said, "Sorry it took me so long. I was in the little girls' room fixing my makeup." Mother Rongway looked at her, shook her head, and said to her, "It took you long enough. If you want my opinion, you do not look any better." She told Toddie, "We will talk about your wedding when I get back." Mother Runnamouth stopped, put her hands on her hips, and asked Mother Rongway, "Just what was that crack about my looks supposed to mean?" Mother Rongway smiled and told her, "I was just kidding. You look just like you did twenty years ago. You was tore up from the floor up then, and you still look the same." Mother Rongway broke out in a big laugh, and Mother Runnamouth shook her fist at her and gave her an evil look as they went out the door.

Meanwhile, Toddie began to clean up and talk to herself again. "Everybody is always telling me what to do. Who cares about Missionary Scareaway's wedding anyway? When Minister Wannado and I get married, that is going to be *the* wedding. People will be talking about my wedding for years. I can see it now, the biggest wedding this town has ever seen." Just then the doorbell rang and interrupted Toddie's train of thought. She got upset and screamed in an angry voice, asking who was at the door. A voice from on the other side of the door yelled back loudly and said, "It is Elder and Sister Backnibbler. We are here for Missionary Scareaway's wedding. Can we come in?" Toddie yelled back loudly and said, "No, and go away. Missionary Scareaway ran away and joined the circus, and her wedding has been canceled." Another voice shouted from on the other side of the door and wanted to know if that was Toddie Rongway. The voiceKnibbler. I used to spank you when you was a little girl. Do not make me come in there and spank you again. Open this door before I get upset."

Toddie slowly opened the door and stood there with both hands on her hips. Very calmly, she asked sister Backnibbler, "Do you really think you can still spank me? I do not think so, but you are welcome to try if you have a death wish." She told them to come in. Elder Backnibbler, trying to be funny, said to Toddie, "I thought it was just a myth, but bigfoot does exist, and what's so amazing is the fact that he lives right here in our town." Sister Backnibbler told him, "You need to stop, because you know bigfoot does not really exist. That is Mother Rongway's granddaughter, Toddie. She is just a little bit bigger than I remember." She leaned over and whispered to Jeffro, "A lot bigger than I remember if you ask me." They both laughed. Toddie called them two religious wannabes and asked them, "Are you two through laughing at my expense?" She then asked, with an attitude, "What do you two want? My grandmother is not home, so you both can leave." Elder Backnibbler, confused as usual, asked his wife, Irene, "Why are we here? We should go somewhere and get something to eat, because I am hungry. I told you to cook before we left home, but you did not listen."

Sister Backnibbler, clearly upset, balled up her fist and shook it at him. She said to him, "You better not embarrass me while we are out. You better not even ask for a drink of water. If you do, it will be on, me and you." She pointed at herself, then at him. Toddie screamed and said, "Excuse me, demon one and demon two. Once again, what do you two want? My grandmother is terribly busy and does not have time to entertain demons, so the two of you need to leave." Elder Backnibbler got an attitude and told Toddie, "Hold up there, Miss Thang. I am not a demon, but I do not know for sure about my wife, Irene. Sometimes I think I see her head rise up off her body and spin around." At that statement, Sister Backnibbler got really upset, grabbed him, and started punching him. She called him a knock-kneed, pigeon-toed, blind-as-a-bat heathen. She said to him, "You are the devil's first illegitimate child, and you have the nerve to call me a demon." She punched him and told him, "Take that!" She punched him again and again and said, "And that, and that." She told him, "I will teach you to call me a demon. When I get through with you, your own mother will not recognize you."

Toddie fell out laughing and said, "Man, that was good." She told Sister Backnibbler, "Punch his lights out. Beat him like he stole something." Elder Backnibbler began to beg and plead. He told his wife, "I am sorry. I did not mean to call you a demon. I made a mistake, and you are not a demon. I meant to say *angel*." Sister Backnibbler stopped punching him, looked at Toddie and told her, "Being married is not that hard. You just have to learn how to speak in a language they understand. You have to learn how to communicate, that is all." Toddie looked at her in disbelief and said, "I don't know about that." Toddie began to laugh and said, "If you ask me, I think you may have gotten the wrong understanding of communication. Maybe you should look that up in another dictionary, because the one you looked in gave you the wrong meaning."

Elder Backnibbler, with relief, agreed with Toddie. He said, "I have been trying to tell her that for years, but every time I say something, she just starts punching me again. I am tired of being her punching bag." Sister Backnibbler, as she got herself together, told him, "The Good Book does say if you spare the rod, you will spoil the heathen, and you know I believe in doing whatever the Good Book says." Toddie, still laughing, apologized. She said, "You two are not demons, you are heathens, and evidently heathens who cannot hear. Read my lips. Once again, why are you two here? It is not a good time, and my grandmother is not here." Sister Backnibbler snapped back at Toddie and said, "Excuse me, your holiness, but evidently you cannot hear either. I was sure I told you that we are here for Missionary Scareaway's wedding. You need to get your hearing checked, because you have a hearing problem."

Suddenly the doorbell rang. Toddie screamed and told her, "You better be glad that doorbell rang," and she went to see who was at the door. She said, "I was about ready to put my foot upside that big head of yours." Elder Backnibbler began to laugh and said, "That would have been a good trick," as he sat down. He said, "I would have liked to see you do that." Sister Backnibbler screamed and told him to shut up as she sat down too. She told him, "Do not get me started in here again. Next time you will not get off so easy." Toddie yelled through the door and said, "Whoever it is, go away. I have enough demons in here already. My grandmother's house is not where the demon convention is being held; it is being held down the street." A voice on the other side of the door yelled back and said, "Hello, it is Evangelist Trying and Deaconess Donothing. We are here for Missionary Scareaway's wedding. Can we come in?"

Toddie began talking to herself again. She said, "I do not know why my grandmother agreed to have this stupid wedding here in the first place." She opened the door and told them to come on in. "The heathen twins are already here," she said, and then sat down. Elder Backnibbler spoke with excitement and relief in his voice. He said to them, "I am sure glad the two of you stopped by. Things were starting to get hot in here. I was about ready to call the fire department." Sister Backnibbler said, "It was not going to get too hot in here. I am an expert at putting out fires. I was about to lay my hands on Toddie and beat some of that devil out of her just like I had to do to you. I can tell you have been delivered since I laid my hands on you." Deaconess Donothing backed up toward the door and talked with a tremble in her voice. She hesitantly told Evangelist Trying, "Maybe we came at an inconvenient time. We can always come back later. I do not want any of those spirits to jump on me. I just had an exorcism, and I do not ever want to go through that again, not in this life." Evangelist Trying agreed and said, "The devil is a liar. All we have to do is put our foot on the devil's head and there is not anything he can do, so do not be scared; we got this." Sister Backnibbler, looking at Toddie, agreed. She then asked Toddie, "Will you come over here where I am so I can put my foot on your head? After all, that song did say to stomp that devil out of you, and I just want to set you free." Toddie became upset and yelled as she got up to leave the room. She told everyone, "I am going to my room before I have to go to jail for mass murder. I am about to flip out in here and kill everybody." She went out of the room and slammed the door behind her. Deaconess Donothing raised her hands and walked around the room. She said, "I do not know about anybody else, but I discern a hostile spirit in this house. I can feel it in the air. It is like a thick fog." Evangelist Trying, mocking Deaconess Donothing, said to her, "I am sure flesh and blood did not reveal that to you. That had to be a divine revelation."

Elder Backnibbler jumped up and put his hand on Deaconess Donothing's shoulder, and with excitement in his voice, he said to her, "I did not know you have the gift of discernment. You are deep,

really deep. I thought I was gifted, but you are authentic." Sister Backnibbler told him, "It does not take discernment to feel the hostility in this house. You must have forgotten whose house we are in. Hostility is just the tip of the iceberg. This house is like a demonic war zone if you ask me." Deaconess Donothing was in deep thought. She told sister Backnibbler that she was right. She said, "When I walked through the door, I knew something was wrong in this house." Then she asked, "Whose house are we in, anyway?" Evangelist Trying threw her hands up and started waving them around. She said to the deaconess, "That right there is what I have been telling you all this time. That is why you do not have a husband, you are braindead."

CHAPTER 10
Things Began to Heat up at Mother's House

Sister Backnibbler put her arm around the deaconess's shoulder and said, "Poor Deaconess Donothing. I did not know you do not have a fully functioning brain. I feel so bad for you. Is there anything I can do?" Deaconess Donothing became upset, and you could hear it in her voice. She told sister Backnibbler, "Just because I forget where I am from time to time, does not mean something is wrong with my brain. It just means I am forgetful, that is all." Elder Backnibbler said he agreed with the deaconess. He said, "Sister Backnibbler keeps telling me I need a brain transplant, and I know there is not anything wrong with my brain. Anyhow, we cannot afford for me to get a brain transplant." Evangelist Trying could not take any more of this, so she changed the conversation. She said to them, "Now that it has been established that everybody in here is a genius, can somebody please tell me where the people are? I thought we were here for a wedding."

Deaconess Donothing, full of excitement, shouted out, "Oh, yes, we are here for Missionary Scareaway's wedding. I do not know about anybody else, but I am here to meet a tall, good-looking, well-built, well-dressed, good-smelling man." Sister Backnibbler began to laugh and told the deaconess, "You might want to make sure he has all his teeth, and more importantly, a job. Not like somebody else I know in the room, sitting over there, who happens to be my husband." Elder

Backnibbler jumped up and got loud. He said, "It is not my fault I got fired. When I got the job, nobody told me I had to work eight hours every day. I had to have some time for myself. They must have thought I was a machine. They must be crazy." Sister Backnibbler got upset at him again. She said to him, "I bet they did not tell you to take three hours for lunch, either. Who ever heard of anybody getting a three-hour lunch break?"

Evangelist Trying started laughing and said, "Not me, but back to this wedding. I do not mean any harm, and Missionary Scareaway is my homegirl, but if she can get a husband, I know I can get one. I was getting somewhat discouraged but not anymore. Miracles do happen." Deaconess Donothing agreed and said, "I know that is right. The Good Book does say that the Lord works in funny ways. I know He had to be laughing when He gave Missionary Scareaway a husband." Elder Backnibbler told the Deaconess, "You can say that again. I saw the boy the other day, and he is one funny-looking brother if you ask me. I could be wrong, but that is just my opinion." Sister Backnibbler looked at him with a surprised look on her face. She said to him, "I hate to be the bearer of bad news, and you are my husband and all, but have you looked in the mirror lately? I would not be talking about somebody else looking funny if I were you." Elder Backnibbler asked her, "Just what are you trying to say? For your information, I look in the mirror every day, so what is your point? I do not get it."

Evangelist Trying interrupted, now somewhat annoyed. She asked, "Would you two please stop fussing long enough to answer my question? Give it a rest already. Are we the only ones here for the wedding?" Very rudely, sister Backnibbler asked her, "Do you see anybody else? Maybe you need glasses, or maybe you are blind in one eye and cannot see out the other one. Which one is it?" Evangelist Trying spun around with a startled look on her face. She shouted at sister Backnibbler, "Hold up, my sister. I am not the one you want to get smart with. I have not had religion that long yet, so the Lord is still working on me. I advise you to take a chill pill before I lay down what religion I do have, then lay you down. Do you feel me?" Deaconess Donothing jumped up and told sister Backnibbler, "You might want to chill. Like the evangelist said, she is not really that saved yet, and she will whip you like you stole something. Just ask me; I know. One time I got the evangelist upset, and my whole life passed before my eyes. You better be careful."

Elder Backnibbler spoke up to defend his wife. He told them, "Wait just a minute. I know my wife may have a few loose screws, and just maybe she does need a good, old-fashioned whipping, but I will not stand here and watch, so I will leave. Call me when Evangelist Trying gets through." Sister Backnibbler was in shock and upset and could not believe what her husband had just said. She told him, "If you move one inch, I will forget you are my husband, and will forget I got religion, and will break every bone in your pitiful-looking body. I am about one minute off you, and that is a skinny minute at that. You better cool it, mister." Just then, Mother Rongway and Mother Runnamouth came in with a bunch of bags. Mother Rongway cheerfully announced that they were back. She said, "We went out to do a little shopping and come back and my house is full of church folk." She asked how they all were doing. She told them, "It is so good to see all of you."

A complete silence came over the house. Everybody was as quiet as a church mouse. Mother Runnamouth looked around confused and asked, "What has been going on in here? It is cold enough in here to put on a pair of long johns and kill a hog." She asked, "What have you all been doing? Why is everybody so quiet? Inquiring minds want to know." Deaconess Donothing spoke up and said, "I cannot speak for everybody else, but I have not been doing anything. I was just sitting here minding my own business." Evangelist Trying could not believe what she was hearing. She got an attitude and said, "The devil is a liar." She said to deaconess Donothing, "To hear you tell it, you never do anything wrong. That is your problem. You are Miss Goody-Two-Shoes. Now I understand where your name comes from: *do nothing!*" Sister Backnibbler agreed and told the evangelist, "You can say that again. I do not know anybody who has never done anything wrong but Deaconess

Donothing. Just being around that woman makes me feel like I am going straight to hell." Elder Backnibbler started laughing and told his wife, "Wait a minute. You can go there if you want to, but I am not going with you. I will stay here until you get back. You are on your own."

Mother Rongway interrupted before they got started again. She told them, "That is enough of that crazy talk. Everybody sit down, and Mother Runnamouth and I will fix some snacks." She asked Mother Runnamouth, "Will you come in the kitchen and give me a hand?" Mother Runnamouth sat down on the couch with her bags and told Mother Rongway, "You can fix them a snack if you want to, but my feet are killing me. All I plan to do is sit here and rest. All that walking got my ankles swelling up." Just then Toddie came into the room and immediately began to cry to her grandmother. With crocodile tears in her eyes, she told her grandmother, "I am so glad you are back. Your church members came in here insulting me and talking about you like a dog. If I did not know better, I would think they did not like you or something. You should have heard the way they were going on. I had to leave the room. I could not take it."

Mother Runnamouth got excited and jumped up off the couch. She said, "Oh, junk. Feet hurting or not, I am getting out of here. World War Three is about to break out, and I do not want to get caught in the crossfire. I will be in the kitchen, and I do not want to be disturbed." She took her bags and left the room in a hurry. Sister Backnibbler jumped up in a panic and began to sweat. Nervously, she told her husband, Jeffro, "We need to go to the store and get Missionary Scareaway a wedding present and get something for my stomach. I do not feel well. We will come back later." Elder Backnibbler told her, "I am confused. I thought you said we were not getting Missionary Scareaway a present right now. When did that change? I do not understand." Sister Backnibbler told him, "Shut up and come on while you are still able to walk," then put a fake grin on her face. She told him, "You do not need to understand; you just need to do what I tell you to do." She took him by his arm and pulled him toward the door so they could leave.

Toddie followed them to the door, trying to get them upset. She asked them, "Why are you guys running now?" And she laughed as they went out the door. She said to them, "I bet you two are not talking all that junk now." Then she shouted, "Run, rabbits, run!" still laughing. Deaconess Donothing saw her chance to suck up, so she wasted no time. In an attempt to suck-up, she told Mother Rongway, "Evangelist Trying and I did not say anything about you because we both know that you are a godly woman. We know everything everybody said about you was a lie. We both know you love everybody, and you are the sweetest person we know." Evangelist Trying told the deaconess, "You can stop sucking up now, but I agree with what you said." She then said to Mother Rongway, "The deaconess is right. We came over here for Missionary Scareaway's wedding, and when we got here, the Backnibblers were already here. We have no idea what they might have said about you before we got here."

Mother Rongway held up both hands and got spiritual. She told them, "I am a changed woman now, and I do not let people worry me anymore. I just want to live so the Lord can use me anytime and anywhere. That is my life now. I just live for the Lord." Toddie was shocked by what she had just heard her devious grandmother say. She laughed and told her, "Earlier today, you were ready to cut somebody, and now you say you are a changed woman. How can you go from being a gangbanger one minute to being a godly woman the next?" She asked her grandmother to explain that one. Mother Rongway looked at her with anger on her face and told her, "Shut up before I put my fist in your mouth. I am a grown woman, and I do not have to answer to you or anybody else." She then told them all, "Excuse me. I am going to the kitchen to help Mother Runnamouth." She left the room and went to the kitchen.

Deaconess Donothing got up, ready to leave, and began to speak nervously. She asked Evangelist Trying, with a tremble in her voice, "Don't you think we should leave and come back later? It is starting to get scary in this house, and I am ready to get out of here." Evangelist

Trying looked at her and asked her, "Are you going to give me some gas money?" She paused with her hands on her hips and waited for a response from Deaconess Donothing. There was no answer. The evangelist said, "I did not think so. Take it easy, and we will be fine. After all, we are covered with the blood, so just calm down." Deaconess Donothing slowly sat back down with her knees knocking and shaking with fear. She told the evangelist, "That is exactly what I am afraid of, us getting covered with blood, our own blood, that is. I do not know about you, but I do not have any blood to waste like that."

Toddie saw a chance to turn up the heat, so she tried to scare Deaconess Donothing some more. She told them, "I am not trying to scare you folks, but it might be better to leave like the deaconess said. You all do not know Rosalee Rongway. That woman will cut you if you rub her the wrong way. You do not want to get on her bad side." At that moment, the doorbell rang. A voice on the other side of the door yelled really loudly and boisterously and said, "Hello! Is there anybody in there, and can somebody open this door? I do not intend to stand out here all day, so I suggest somebody get a move on." Evangelist Trying asked, "Who in God's name is that? Somebody better hurry up and open that door. Whoever that is out there sounds like they are about ready to huff and puff and blow this house down."

Toddie said, "That sounds like Evangelist Scareaway, and you are right, she just might blow the house down. There is one thing I know about that woman: she is definitely full of hot air." Toddie screamed at the top of her voice and said, "Just a minute! I am coming; just do not blow the house down." She opened the door and saw that it was not only Evangelist Scareaway, but June Bug, her son, was with her also. Very arrogant, Evangelist Scareaway told Toddie, "It took you long enough to come to the door. Can we come in? We do not have all day to hang around here; we have other things to do." Toddie responded in her best country voice and told them, "Y'all come on in now, y'all hear. Take y'all shoes off and sit a spell. Y'all want me to fetch y'all a glass of water?" June Bug replied and told her, "Spare me the theatricals.

I made my mother come back over here to apologize for the way she acted earlier, but we can just leave. We do not need any more drama." Toddie told them, "Do not let me stop you. By all means, leave. I do not want it to be said that Toddie Rongway kept you from your destiny. If you two are destined to leave, then leave."

Evangelist Trying intervened. She told the two of them to hold up. She said, "I do not know what the problem is, but everybody seems to be at each other's throats. Everybody needs to calm down and get a grip. Whatever it is, it cannot be that serious." Deaconess Donothing agreed and said, "Evangelist Trying is right. I thought this was supposed to be a happy occasion. It is not every day that Missionary Scareaway can find somebody dumb enough to marry her." At that moment, the deaconess realized what she had just said and looked around in fear. Evangelist Scareaway got angry and looked at the deaconess with piercing eyes and began to yell. She said, "Somebody needs to find me some anointing oil so I can anoint myself. I need the Lord to strengthen me one more time. This deaconess has insulted my niece, and it is time to throw down. Come on, Deaconess Donothing, and show me what you got."

Brother June Bug rolled up his sleeves and spit in his hands, ready for battle. He told his mother, "You were absolutely right about these weird people. I thought we came over here to apologize, but these people do not need an apology; they need a good, old-fashioned Holy Ghost whipping. I know it is only the two of us, but the Good Book did say where there are two in agreement, He will help them out." Toddie got excited and said, "That sounds like a good deal to me. I am going to do like *The Bible* said: whip you two in season and out of season. I am going to lay both of my hands on both of you. Come on, June the Bug and Evangelist Scary Face."

Evangelist Trying shouted loudly and told them, "Everybody needs to calm down. What is going on, and has everyone lost their minds? I thought all of you were church people, but evidently I must be wrong. From what I can see, you all need to go back and be dipped at least seven times." Toddie said, "I never told anybody that I caught religion or anything else. Seeing the way the Scareaways are acting, they may have caught something, but they did not catch any kind of religion." Deaconess Donothing, scratching her head, replied, "I know I caught something, and I think it was religion, but now I am not sure. Maybe it was the flu." Evangelist Scareaway calmed down, held her head back, stuck out her chest, and began to brag. She said, "I know I got good religion. My grandmother had it, her great-grandmother had it, and they passed it down to me. Nobody can tell me what I do not have. I inherited my religion."

June Bug, still upset, said, "Personally I do not care what Grandmother passed down, and personally I do not care what the rest of you caught or think you caught. One thing I do know for sure is somebody is about to catch a right hook and a left uppercut." He threw a few punches to demonstrate his skills. Evangelist Scareaway tried to calm him down. Now trying to be motherly, she told him, "It is okay, son. Now breathe. That's it, breathe. Take a deep breath and let it out. Calm down, because these people are not worth you having a stroke. We will let the Lord fight our battle." Evangelist Trying looked at Evangelist Scareaway and said, "I am so glad you calmed that demon down. I did not want to revert back to my street days and turn this place out. I know I do not look like it now, but back in the day, I banged heads every weekend." Now, Toddie did not feel that way. She told Evangelist Scareaway, "You do not have to calm him down at all. I have some medicine right here in both my fists that will make him lie down and take a long nap, guaranteed." Deaconess Donothing jumped up, got loud and said, "Yes, what she said." Then she told Toddie, "Go ahead and tell them, because I have your back. In fact, I will be back over here behind the couch if you need me." She backed up behind the couch. Evangelist Scareaway told everybody, "You all need to back up off my son. The spirit is not through with him yet. He is still in the oven being worked on." Evangelist Trying replied and told her, "You are right about one thing: June Bug has a spirit, all right, an evil spirit.

I think somebody needs to lay hands on him and cast that demon out before it is too late."

With that said, Evangelist Trying called for Mother Rongway, who was in the kitchen. Toddie saw another chance to sell wolf tickets, so she jumped on it. She told them, "If I were in your shoes, right now I would be afraid, be very afraid. When Rosalee Rongway comes through that door, it is all over. You two might as well say your goodbyes right now." Evangelist Scareaway got brave. She said, "I am not afraid of the grim reaper. I have already made my home-going plans. I told them when I die, bury me deep. I want two kegs of molasses at my feet. I want two cakes of corn bread in my hand. I plan to sop my way to the promised land." Then she shouted, "Oh, glory!"

Toddie and Evangelist Trying both looked at Evangelist Scareaway, then looked at each other and started laughing. Toddie said to her, "I know you are a hillbilly, and try to pretend you are spiritual, but you have mental issues. Who ever heard of anybody sopping their way to the promised land or any other land. That does not even make any sense." Then Toddie laughed again. Evangelist Trying, still laughing, said, "I agree with Toddie; that makes no sense." Deaconess Donothing spoke up, trembling, and said, "You all seem to be having fun, but I do not know about anybody else, but I am scared out of my socks. I experienced the wrath of Mother Rongway once, and it was not pretty." Evangelist Scareaway gave Evangelist Trying a dirty look and shook her head, showing disapproval. She told her, "You had the gall to call my son a demon, then called Lucifer's mama to come in here."

She yelled and told June Bug, "Come on so we can get out of this demonic house before I backslide and really hurt somebody. These people do not know who they are messing with." June Bug agreed and said, "You tell them, Mother. They do not want you to backslide, because they would not like you if you did." Just as they went out the door, Mother Rongway came into the room. She asked, "Did somebody call me?" as she came through the door. She told them, "Mother Runnamouth had that music up so loud in the kitchen, I could barely hear myself think." Evangelist Trying said, "Yes, I called you. There were a couple of demons in here acting up, but when I called you, they went back to wherever demons go." Toddie jumped in and told her grandmother, "Evangelist Scareaway and June Bug were just here. You should have seen the way they were acting. I have never seen those two act like that before."

CHAPTER 11

Minister Wannado Shocks Toddie and Mother Rongway

Mother Rongway held up both hands and looked up. She said, "That woman is trying her best to make me lose my religion. The devil is a liar." Deaconess Donothing, being the hair brain that she was, said, "I think this will be a suitable time for everybody to gather around and sing a happy song. Who is with me?" Everybody gave her a look as if to say, *Are you kidding me?* Mother Rongway, looking at her, asked, "did you just fall off the fruit truck this morning, or did you fall off it a long time ago?" Evangelist Trying fell back on her chair laughing. She told Mother Rongway, "Not only did she fall off the truck, but I think the truck ran over her too." Everybody in the room began to laugh. Deaconess Donothing got upset. She did not find that funny. She said, "I know I forget stuff sometimes, but I am sure I would remember falling off a truck." Just then Toddie said, "I am going back to my room to lie back down," and Mother Runnamouth came into the room, fussing. She shouted at Mother Rongway and said, "I thought I came over here to help you. I did not know I would be doing all the work. My feet are hurting, and I am tired." She sat down. Evangelist Trying volunteered her services. She told Mother Rongway, "If you need somebody to help in the kitchen, I do not mind giving you a hand. Remember, I cook all the time." Mother Rongway, in her sweet, motherly voice, told her, "No, thank you. Mother Runnamouth and I can manage it. I have tasted your cooking, but I appreciate the offer."

Mother Runnamouth jumped up in a panic and said, "I am going back in the kitchen. It is getting too hot up in this room again for me. People are getting burned all over the place." She and Mother Rongway left the room and went back into the kitchen. Evangelist Trying stood there, angry, with her mouth open in disbelief. She gasped and said, "I know that old woman did not just try to get smart with me." She looked up and began to sing the "Sticks and Stones" rhyme. Meanwhile, deaconess Donothing stood there in fear that Mother Rongway was going to come back through that door. She whispered and told Evangelist Trying, "I do not know about you, but I think it is time for us to leave before Mother Rongway comes back in here. We came over here for Missionary Scareaway's wedding, but we did not come over here to be insulted like that." Evangelist Trying told the deaconess, "You have never lied. The Bible does say if you resist the devil, she will flee, but I am having a tough time resisting knocking her false teeth out, so we better leave. Maybe we will come back for the wedding, or maybe not. The way I am feeling right now, I do not know."

They left, and Mother Rongway came back into the room. She said, "Thank God my house is finally empty for a little while." She called Toddie and told her, "Come in here and straighten up a little. Minister Wannado called and said he is on his way over here, and I know you would not want him to see this house in a mess like it is now." Toddie came into the room, and excitedly yelled, "Hallelujah! Finally, my future husband is on his way over here. I knew he could not stay away from me much longer. I have that magnetic kind of love that he just cannot resist." Mother Rongway started laughing and said, "I do not know about that magnetic stuff, but you better hurry up because he said he was just around the corner and will be here any minute." Mother Rongway went out of the room. Toddie screamed with excitement. She said, "Minister Wannado makes my liver quiver."

Just then the doorbell rang, and Toddie called out in her sweet voice and asked who was at the door. Minister Wannado yelled back in his preacher voice from outside the door and said, "It is the right reverend Minister Wannado. I am here for Missionary Scareaway's wedding. Is it all right if I come in?" Toddie opened the door, still excited, called his name and said he was her future husband. She then told him, "It was about time you got here. What took you so long?" She called him *baby* and told him to come in. Minister Wannado came in, along with his real fiancée, Sister Knowsall. He said to Toddie, "You remember Sister Knowsall." Sister Knowsall said to Toddie, "I have not seen you in a long time. You still look the same. How have you been doing?" Toddie, with an attitude, said, "I was doing a lot better before I saw you, and what are you doing with my future husband? You have some explaining to do." Sister Knowsall got upset and yelled, "The devil is a liar." Then she asked Minister Wannado, "Do you want to straighten out Miss Thang, or should I? You know I will." Toddie put both hands on her hips and moved her head from side to side with an attitude. She said to sister Knowsall, "If anyone needs to be straightened out, it is you. Minister Wannado have been in love with me for a long time, but we just never told anyone." She then called minister Wannado baby and asked him, "isn't that right."

Minister Wannado looked at Toddie and said, "I've told you a hundred times there is nothing between the two of us, so you need to stop this nonsense." He started to say, "You are too", then stopped and said, "you know," but Toddie stopped him before he could finish. Instead, she asked him, "I am too what?" Now, with a serious attitude, she told him, "You better not even part your lips to say what I think you are trying to say. Future husband or not, I will punch you in the face." Sister Knowsall spoke up, moving her neck from side to side, and said, "I think he was saying you are not his type." Then she told Toddie, "If you really want to know, you are too . . ." Minister Wannado interrupted before Sister Knowsall could finish her statement and shouted, "Too young! Yes, that is it,. You are too young for me. That is what I was about to say." Toddie screamed and called him a two-timing, low-down, jack-leg preacher. She told him, "You know you are my husband. I had a dream that you are, and that is all the proof I need."

Sister Knowsall got sarcastic and told Toddie, "Now I understand," attempting to do a Martin Luther King imitation. She told her, "You had a dream that one day you and Minister Wannado would be together, but I do not think so. That was just those collard greens and pork chops you keep eating all the time. If you do not stop eating that kind of stuff, you will keep having those bad dreams, but I am your worst nightmare, so do not push me." Minister Wannado, in his preacher persona, said, "Do not let that demon take control of your minds. You both should be fighting the devil, not one another, but if the Lord leads you to fight one another, you two have my blessings. Let the battle begin." Toddie looked at the two of them and said, "I will settle this problem. You two lovebirds do not know who you are messing with."

She looked toward the kitchen and called Mother Rongway. She yelled for her and said, "I need you to come in here right this minute." Sister Knowsall looked at her and told her, "I guess you are happy now. You just had to call the drama queen of all drama queens. That just shows how immature you really are. You had to call your grandmother because you are not woman enough to fight your own battles. I rest my case." Mother Rongway rushed into the room in a panic, shouting, asking Toddie, "What is wrong? Are you all right?" Then she saw Minister Wannado and Sister Knowsall. She said, "Praise the Lord, Minister Wannado and Sister Knowsall. How is everybody doing? I did not know the two of you were in here." Minister Wannado spoke up in his preacher voice and said, "Praise the Lord, Mother Rongway. The Lord is my shepherd, and He has given me what I wanted." Toddie got excited again and said to sister Knowsall, "You see, I told you Minister Wannado wanted me, not you. I do not have any bad feelings toward you or anything, because you just did not know who you were competing with, so you need to back off."

Sister Knowsall looked at Toddie and with a stern voice, told her, "I was trying to spare your feelings, but you give me no other choice. For your information, Minister Wannado asked me to marry him, and I said yes, and I have the ring to prove it." She showed Toddie her engagement ring. Toddie screamed as loudly as she could, then fainted and fell back on the couch. Mother Rongway was just as shocked and almost lost her composure but pulled herself together. She screamed, "What?", Then she said, "I meant to say congratulations. When is the big day, and why was I not told about your engagement? I need to be kept informed about something important like this. This is big news." Minister Wannado said, "We have not set a date yet, so we have not told anyone yet. After all, this is the first time I have seen you since I popped the big question." Sister Knowsall spoke up, glowing with excitement. She told Mother Rongway, "Not only that, but I have been on cloud nine ever since he asked me, and I did not want to spoil Missionary Scareaway's wedding, so I told Minister Wannado not to tell anyone just yet."

Minister Wannado asked Mother Rongway, "Where is Missionary Scareaway? She asked me to meet her here so we could rehearse for her funeral." Then he realized what had come out of his mouth and said, "That was a slip of the tongue. I meant to say, "her wedding." Mother Rongway looked over her glasses at Minister Wannado. She said, "Same difference if you ask me," trying not to laugh. She said, "Either way, your life is over." Sister Knowsall said, "I do not care what anybody says. The Lord has blessed me with the man of my dreams, and I do not plan to let anybody, or anything, spoil that." Minister Wannado, in his preacher voice, shouted and said, "The Good Book does say, 'He may not give you a man when you want one, but He will give you one on time,' or something like that."

At that moment, Toddie woke up from her fainting episode and tried to figure out what had just happened to her. Still not completely coherent, she asked, "What happened? I think I had a bad dream. I dreamed Sister Knowsall said Minister Wannado asked her to marry him. Somebody please tell me I was dreaming." Mother Rongway spoke up and told her, "You were not dreaming. It looks like these two lovebirds are planning to jump the broom. I believe we will soon be having another wedding. There must be an epidemic going around. Suddenly everybody is getting married." Suddenly Toddie jumped up from the couch, upset; she screamed and began talking loudly. She told them, "I am going to my room and jump out the window and kill myself. If anybody comes looking for me, I will be outside my window with a broken neck."

Sister Knowsall began to laugh and told Toddie, "I hate to bust your bubble, but your window is only about three or four feet from the ground. If you jump out of it, the only thing that can happen is maybe you will get a twisted ankle. If you want to do it right, maybe you should jump off the roof. I am sure that will do the trick." Minister Wannado tried to intervene. He said to them, "You two should not be fighting in Mother Rongway's house. You should know better than that. I suggest you both go outside where there is plenty of room, and let the Lord use you." Sister Knowsall smiled and told minister Wannado, "You have so much wisdom and your sense of humor is one of the reasons I said yes when you asked me to marry you. You make me laugh all the time." Mother Rongway started laughing and agreed he was funny. She said, "I was thinking he just looked like a clown, but now see I was wrong."

Once again the doorbell rang, and Mother Rongway went to the door. She opened the door and discovered that it was Missionary Scareaway and June Bug. Missionary Scareaway, all happy and bubbly, spoke and said, "Cousin June Bug and myself are here for my wedding rehearsal. May we come in?" Mother Rongway said, "It is one of my girls, Missionary Scareaway, along with brother June Bug. Come on in. Minister Wannado and Sister Knowsall are already here." She asked them to excuse her for a minute. She said, "I need to make sure Toddie is okay. Everyone sit down and make yourselves at home." Mother Rongway went out of the room and everybody sat down. Missionary Scareaway asked Minister Wannado and Sister Knowsall, "How are you folks doing? Do you remember my cousin June Bug from down South?" Sister Knowsall said, "Of course we do." She told him, "It is good to see you again."

Brother June Bug tried to flirt with Sister Knowsall. He told her, "It is good to see you, with your good-looking self." Then he asked Minister Wannado, "How are you doing? You still look the same. You do not look one day older than you did the last time I saw you." Minister Wannado, in a serious tone of voice and with a serious look on his face, told June Bug, "Before you get a heavy anointing and put your foot in your mouth, Sister Knowsall and I are engaged, and I am doing just fine, thanks for asking." Brother June Bug realized he may have gone too far, and he offered somewhat of an apology. "Oops, my bad," he said grinning. "I did not mean any harm. I thought she was fair game and did not know she was already spoken for." He told minister Wannado, "You are the man." Missionary Scareaway congratulated them and said, "it is about time. What took you two so long? Everybody knew that you two were meant for each other. If there ever were two people who belong together, it is you two." Minister Wannado agreed.

At that moment, Minister Wannado jumped up and began to preach. He began to moan and said, "I just want to let everybody know how the Lord has blessed me. If you wait on the Lord, He will give you a good woman or a good man." Then he asked, "Can I get an *amen*? Can I get a *hallelujah*? Can I get a *Thank you, Jesus*? Can I get a *You go, boy*?" Brother June Bug laughed and said, "I can see Wannado has not changed. I can see he is still ready to preach at the drop of a dime." Minister Wannado, still in his preacher mode, told him, "The Good Book does say, 'Be ye instantaneous when it is your season, and be ye instantaneous when it is not your season.' That is why I stay ready. I never know when my season might pop up." Sister Knowsall jumped up. excited, and said, "That is another reason I said yes when he asked me to marry him. He is just like instant coffee. He can get fired up in a minute." Missionary Scareaway said, "I know that is right. If you give Minister Wannado half a chance, he will give you a full-blown sermon. There is one thing I have to say about that preacher man: he is full of the word and does not mind spitting it out."

CHAPTER 12

A WEDDING REHEARSAL UNLIKE ANY OTHER

Just then the doorbell rang, and Mother Rongway's daughter, Lula Bell, opened the door and came in before anyone could go to the door. She shouted hello and asked if anybody was home as she came in. At that moment she saw everybody and asked, "Why are all of you in my mother's house, and where is my mother?" Brother June Bug got up, moved to the other side of the room, and said, "Just when you thought things could not get any worse, in comes Hurricane Lula Bell. There will be trouble now; we can count on that. There goes the neighborhood if you ask me." Missionary Scareaway, with excitement still in her voice, told Lula Bell, "Do not pay any attention to my cousin June Bug, because I am sure he is just joking. Where have you been? I have not seen you in years." Sister Knowsall stood up, also excited to see Sister Lula Bell. She said to her, "I also have not seen you in years. You are a welcome sight. How have you been doing? You look good."

Minister Wannado stood up with a sheepish grin on his face and spoke in his preacher voice. "When I think of the goodness of the Lord, and all the good things He has done to you." Sister Knowsall interrupted him before he could finish his sentence. Very calmly, she told him, "Since you cannot seem to keep your mind on Jesus, I think it will be best for you to keep your eyes on me. I do not want you to have to use a seeing-eye dog on our wedding day. What do you think?" With an attitude, Lula Bell told them, "I already spoke. I know I look good, and I have not seen all of you in years either, but nobody answered my question. Once again, what are all of you doing in my mother's house, and where is my mother?" Brother June Bug got some courage, spoke up with an attitude, and said to her, "Excuse me, Miss Pistol. We did not know you were loaded. We are here to rehearse for Missionary Scareaway's wedding if that is all right with you."

Missionary Scareaway got an attitude and pointed at Sister Lula Bell. Shouting, she told her, "We know this is your mother's house, but you do not have to come up in here showing your true colors. I do not have but so much patience, so we can take it outside. It is not a good day for all this drama, and I am about two seconds from slapping the taste out of your mouth, so do not push it." Minister Wannado, once again in his preacher voice, told them, "Do not spoil the happy occasion. But I do just want to let everybody know, I just happen to be running a two-for-one special at this moment. I will do a wedding and a funeral for one low price of just $59.95, but that will not last much longer, so you two better take advantage of it while it is hot."

Sister Knowsall tried to calm everybody down. She told them, "Wait a minute, and Minister Wannado is right. It is a happy occasion because Missionary Scareaway is getting married, and Minister Wannado and I are engaged, so everyone should calm down." Sister Lula Bell was shocked, and looking at Minister Wannado, she said to him, "You low-down, two-timing, no-good preacher. You told me that the two of us were going to get married. Now you are engaged to Sister Knowsall. What is up with that?" Brother June Bug looked at Missionary Scareaway and spoke quietly. He told her, "I could be wrong, but, Houston, we have a problem." She told him he had never lied. She said, "Looks like the preacher man got some explaining to do to get out of this one. I hope for his sake he has a good explanation." Sister Knowsall looked at Minister Wannado with tears in her eyes, trying not to cry. "Minister Wannado," she said with pain in her voice, and in her heart. She said to him, "Please tell me that is not true.

I trusted you, so please tell me that you are not a two-timing liar. My heart cannot take that."

In a panic, Minister Wannado tried to explain. He told her, "I do not remember saying anything like that, but if I did, I must have been half-drunk, I mean half asleep. Besides, that is Mother Rongway's daughter, and you know Mother Rongway is a professional liar." Sister Lula Bell told him, "That is enough about my mother. I know my mother does not tell the truth all the time, but she is not a professional liar. She can very well be an amateur liar, but she is not a professional liar, so you need to drop that." Brother June Bug told Lula Bell, "You need to stop. They are not talking about somebody else's mother; they are talking about your mother, Mother Rosalee Rongway. She lies so much she does not even believe anything she says herself." Missionary Scareaway yelled loudly. She told them, "We are here to rehearse for my wedding. I know that may not have much meaning to anyone else, but it means the world to me. Can we drop all this drama and rehearse?" Sister Knowsall, looking at missionary Scareaway with sympathy, told her, "I do not mean any disrespect, but I have to get to the bottom of this mess."

At that point she looked at Minister Wannado again with piercing eyes and demanded an explanation. She called him by his name, Buster, and told him, "You have a lot of explaining to do, and you have about thirty seconds to do it in, so I suggest you get started." At that point, Minister Wannado got down on his knees and begged with everything in him. He told her, "You know you are my all and all, the love of my life, and my dream come true. You are the only woman I have ever asked to be my wife. You must believe me. Lula Bell is lying. She is not even my type. I would never do anything to hurt you, and you need to believe me." Sister Lula Bell started laughing and said, "I was just playing. Minister Wannado never asked me to marry him. I was just messing with him. He is all yours, and you can have him all to yourself."

Sister Knowsall got upset and started crying. She asked Lula Bell, "How could you do that to me? You are a cold and heartless woman, and I do not like you at all. I should come over there and punch you in your face. When I told you that you looked good, I was lying. You are tore up from the floor up." At that moment, Brother June Bug decided to stand up and be a man. He got loud and told Sister Knowsall he had her back. He looked at Sister Lula Bell and called her Miss Thang. He told her, "I have never hit a woman before, but I think I am about to start. That was low-down and dirty, and I think you need to crawl out of this room before somebody has to carry you out. I am not what you call a violent man, but you done went too far, and somebody needs to put you in your place." Missionary Scareaway, screaming as loud as she could, asked, "Can we all just get along? I just came here for the wedding rehearsal and nothing else."

Minister Wannado, getting up off his knees, said, "Amen, amen. Can we get on with the rehearsal before I have a nervous breakdown? For a minute there, I thought my heart was about to explode." He told Sister Lula Bell, "You need to leave, because you are bad news." Sister Knowsall took Minister Wannado's hand and apologized. She told him, "You are right, and I am so sorry I doubted your loyalty. I will never doubt your love again." She gave him a kiss on his cheek. Sister Lula Bell looked around at everybody looking at her and said, "I know when I am not welcome." She got upset and told them, "I am going in the kitchen before I lose my temper and really hurt somebody. You all must have forgotten who my mother is. The Rongways do not take any mess, so you all are lucky." She left the room and went into the kitchen.

Again, the doorbell rang, and Missionary Scareaway went to the door. She said, "I hope that is Deacon and Sister Aintwright. Maybe we can finally get started with the wedding rehearsal." She opened the door, and it was Deacon and sister Aintwright. Cheerfully, she told them to come on in. She said, "I am so glad you guys could make it." They both spoke, and Sister Aintwright told her, "I am sorry it took us so long to get here, but you know how slow Cletus is." They said, "Praise the Lord, everybody," and everybody spoke. Suddenly, the deacon realized what his wife had said. He got loud and said, "I was not the one who was the holdup. You took forever trying to find that broke-down wig you have on." Sister Aintwright sternly told Cletus, "Do not start with me. I am not in the mood to listen to you running off at the mouth. I know you do not want me to go off on you in front of all these people, because you know that I will."

Minister Wannado spoke up in his preacher voice. "Husband and wife should not be fighting one another. You should be fighting against Satan and his demons, which are in the kitchen at this moment." Then he asked, "Can I get an *Amen*? Can I get a *hallelujah*? Can I get a *Thank you, Jesus*?" Brother June Bug agreed and told him, "You can say that again. This house is full of demons. There are enough demons in this house to hold a demon convention." Sister Knowsall told him, "I know that is right. I believe this house is the place the devil and his demons meet to plan what they are going to do every day. This house is demon central." Deacon Aintwright looked around and told her, "That is deep. Did we miss something? Is there something going on in here that we should know about? If so, somebody needs to speak up. I do not play around with demons. I have seen what Mother Rongway can do." He pauses, then said, "I meant, 'what demons can do.'"

Sister Aintwright spoke up and said, "Evidently something must be going on in here, because everybody sounds so serious. Does anybody want to fill us in? If we have to fight demons, I need to get prayed up right quick." By then, Missionary Scareaway had had enough and became angry. With rage in her voice, she loudly asked, "Can we please get on with my wedding rehearsal? I am getting married in a few hours, and I want to at least go over the ceremony. At the rate we are going, there will not be a wedding and I will become an old maid." Minister Wannado, once again in his preacher voice, started preaching and said, "Members of the Rongway First Liberation Church, we did come here today to participate, not to procrastinate, but to associate, not to alienate, but to congratulate, not to opinionate, but to appreciate, not to alleviate, but to stimulate, not to aggravate, but to facilitate, not to simulate." Then he asked, "Can I get an *amen*?"

At that point, everyone looked at Minister Wannado with confusion on their faces. Brother June Bug interrupted and asked Minister Wannado, "Were you trying to make a point or just showing off your rhyming skills?" Sister Knowsall told them, "You all just do not understand Minister Wannado like I do. He is just deep like that. Sometimes he will begin to rhyme and get so caught up in it he does not know when to stop. I believe he can go on for an hour if I do not stop him." Deacon Aintwright got excited and told Sister Knowsall, "You are right about that. Minister Wannado is one of the deepest brothers I know. He is so deep, you have to go deep-sea diving just to get on his level. If the boy got any deeper, nobody would be able to understand him. Now that is deep." They high fived each other. Sister Aintwright sarcastically said, "Yes, he is deep, all right. Can we get back to the rehearsal? At this rate, we will be here all day." Then she asked Missionary Scareaway, "Where is Brother Moanback?" The missionary replied, "He had some last-minute stuff to take care of, so he will not be able to make it. He told me to ask Deacon Aintwright to stand in for him if that is okay with you and the deacon."

Deacon Aintwright jumped at the chance to be in the spotlight, if only for a brief moment. He told her, "No problem. I will be glad to do it." He stuck out his chest and said, "Brother Moanback knew I would be the right man for the job. When you say, 'stand in for him,' what exactly does that mean?" Missionary Scareaway told him, "It is quite simple. All you have to do is just stand here beside me and repeat whatever Minister Wannado tells us to say. Do you understand?" He said, "No problem; I can manage that. I was thinking maybe I would have to kiss the bride or something." Sister Aintwright looked at him with a look of disapproval on her face and said, "I do not think so, Mister Lover Boy wannabe, and do not stand so close together either. I usually do not trust other sisters with my man, but since it is a special occasion, I will make an exception this one time, so you better not go overboard."

Again, Minister Wannado spoke up in his preacher voice and said, "Dearly beloved, we have come here today so that this man and this woman can get a holy hookup." Then he asked, "Can I get an *Amen*?" They all said, "Amen." Sister Aintwright, sounding terribly upset, shouted in her high-pitched voice, "Hold up! Stop the music, Minister Wannado. I object!" She said, "I do not like that one bit. My husband already has a holy hookup with me." Minister Wannado looked at Brother Aintwright and told him, "Wait just one minute. The devil is a liar. How dare you try to get a holy hookup with this sister, and you already have another holy hookup? I cannot do this because it is against my hypocritical oath." Sister Knowsall started smiling and said, "That is my man. That is another reason I said yes when he asked me to marry him. He has such ambitious standards. He is everything any woman would be proud to have for a husband, and he is all mine."

Missionary Scareaway shook her head in disbelief as she looked at them all. She told them, "Wait a minute. Did you all fall down and bump your heads this morning? We are only rehearsing; it is not real. Deacon Aintwright is just standing in for Brother Moanback. He is not trying to get another holy hookup with me." Brother June Bug began laughing. He told them, "You guys call us country folk, but this beats all I have ever seen. I have seen some weird people before, but you all have to be from another planet." Deacon Aintwright told him, "That very well could be. I do not know about anybody else in here, but I heard that women are from Venus and men are from mars." Sister Aintwright, with a big smile on her face, told him, "I do not know about that, but you have to be from the planet Krypton because you know you are my superman."

Deacon Aintwright stuck out his chest and began to strut around like a proud rooster. He got excited and said, "That is what I am talking about. Go ahead, sweet thang, and preach the gospel while I listen. Missionary Scareaway is nice and all, but you are my sweet thang, my Lois Lane every day of the week. Nobody can take your place, not even Wonder Woman herself." Brother June Bug put his finger in his mouth and told them, "Do not make me throw up. You two are about as romantic as a root canal. Listening to you two makes me glad I am not married." Minister Wannado could not help himself. He wanted to preach so badly that every time he opened his mouth, a mini sermon came out. So, in his usual style, in his preacher voice, he told everybody, "Please take a chill pill and let me do my thang while I am closed in my right mind and the blood is still running warm in my veins." Then he asked, "Can I get an *Amen?*"

Sister Aintwright shrugged her shoulders and said, "Whatever. I am only glad we are only pretending. It took me a long time to train Cletus, and I do not want all my hard work to be wasted. If I have to start training him again, I will get me a puppy instead." Minister Wannado, still in his preacher voice, told her, "That is understandable." Then he asked, "Where was I before I was so rudely interrupted?" He paused a moment to collect his thoughts and remember where he was, before continuing. He said, "Marriage is like an institution. Once you get in it, you get stuck. Even if that woman cannot cook, will not clean the house, will not comb her nappy head, will not cut the grass, will not wash the car . . ." Sister Knowsall looked at him like she thought he had lost his mind and told him, "Hold up and stop right there before you say something you will regret." She said, "Put the dog and cat out, and Katy, bar the door," looking around the room at everybody. She told him, "I know you do not expect me to do all that. If you do, we have a problem. You do not need a wife; you need a robot."

Missionary Scareaway laughed and said, "I know that is right, and it better be a male robot, because even a female robot will not do all that." She told Minister Wannado, "You will be better off marrying a cleaning company and be satisfied." Missionary Scareaway and Sister Knowsall high-fived each other. Brother June Bug began to question Missionary Scareaway about her decision to get married. He asked her, "Are you sure you want to get married? I know I am a man and all, but these brothers sound like they have a few issues if you ask me. If this is a look at what being married is like, you might want to rethink the whole thing." She told him, "Brother Moanback isn't like that," and she got all happy and warm inside. She said, "He told me if I keep the grass cut and the cars washed, I will not have to cook or clean the house. Now that is what I call a good man."

Brother June Bug, laughing, told her, "That is great, if that is what you believe. I guess Brother Moanback will be doing all the housework. Remind me not to ever go to your house. That sounds like a disaster waiting to happen. I do not know Brother Moanback, but I know you." Missionary Scareaway gave him an evil look and asked him, "Just what are you trying to say?" It was clear to see she was upset. Brother June Bug told her, "There is no reason for you to get upset. We are just talking among friends." Deacon Aintwright got upset and tried to stand up to his wife. He shouted her name and said to her, "All the time we have been together, you have not been doing your wifely duties. You had me washing the car and mowing the lawn when you should have been doing it all the time." Sister Aintwright screamed, "What?" as she walked toward her husband. She told him, "I know you are not insinuating I cut the grass and wash the car? Please tell me that is not what you are saying. If it is, I will drive you to the hospital and sign you in myself, because you must have lost your mind."

Minister Wannado interrupted them again. He told them, "Hold on, children of the Lord or the devil. I am not sure which one at this point. We should finish the wedding rehearsal so we all can get out of here in one piece. I have the feeling if we stay here much longer, instead of a wedding, there might be a divorce and a funeral." Sister Knowsall looked at him and rolled her eyes. She said to him, "Okay, but me and you will finish our conversation later. Evidently we have a lot more to talk about than I thought." Minister Wannado tried to suck up, so he told her, "Okay, honey dumpling, whatever you say. Now, where was I?" Then he remembered. Then he asked, "Do you, Deacon Aintwright, Brother Moanback's stand-in, take thee, Missionary Scareaway, Missionary Moanback-to-be, for better or for worse?" Deacon Aintwright paused to think before he answered. He said, "Reverend, I will take her for worse because I already have better," as he threw Bertha Mae some kisses. Sister Aintwright got excited and told him to say it. She told him, "I know you are talking right. You can put that on the six o'clock news, and I am the best thing since toilet paper." At that point, Brother June Bug had heard enough to make him sick to his stomach. He asked, "Will somebody please get me a barf bag before I throw up on the floor?"

Sister Knowsall told him, "I am with you on that one. I believe Sister Aintwright had her wig on too tight. She was starting to talk crazy, and you are right, it was sickening." Sister Aintwright got an attitude and snapped back. She smirked and said, "I cannot help it if I have it like that, and I certainly cannot help the fact that everybody is jealous of me. It is not my fault." Minister Wannado spoke up again in his preacher voice before things got too far out of hand. Once again he said, "Members of the Rongway First Liberation Church, can everyone stop all this drama so we can finish this funeral?" He paused and said, "My bad. I meant this wedding rehearsal." Missionary Scareaway again got loud and was upset. She said to them, "The way things are going, I will be too old to get married by the time we get this wedding rehearsal together. I am starting to think that Brother Moanback and I should just go down to the jailhouse and get married."

Minister Wannado agreed but said, "I do believe you meant courthouse," and continued with the rehearsal. He said, "Missionary Scareaway, Missionary Moanback-to-be, do you take Deacon 'Already Got a Hookup' Aintwright for better or for worse?" Missionary Scareaway scratched her head and thought for a moment. She said, "I guess I will have to take him for better. From what I can see at this moment, they certainly do not come any worse." She then told Minister Wannado, "Thank you, and I have to go get dressed." Now excited again, she told everyone, "I am getting married in a few hours." Brother June Bug, releasing a sigh of relief, said, "Thank the Lord this so-called rehearsal is over. I hope your wedding ceremony turns out better than this rehearsal did." Sister Knowsall agreed and told him, "You are right about that. If your wedding is anything like this rehearsal was, it will be the worst wedding in history. Everybody's wedding day is incredibly special."

Meanwhile, Deacon Aintwright still stood with a confused look on his face, until finally he expressed what he was thinking. He asked Missionary Scareaway, "Just what did you mean when you said they do not come any worse? Nobody talks about me like that but my Bertha Mae." Missionary Scareaway told him, "You will figure it out," and she headed toward the door. She said, "I must be going. I will see you all later at my wedding." She told June Bug to come on, and they left. Sister Aintwright assured her husband it was all right. She told him, "Do not worry about what Missionary Scareaway said. I took you for worse until I can find better, but I have not found anybody yet, so you are still good." Now Deacon Aintwright was more confused than before. He stood there looking at his wife and shaking his head. When he finally replied, he said to her, "I am not even going to ask you what you mean by that. I am sure I am better off not knowing."

CHAPTER 13

MINISTER WANNADO SHOWED HIS PREACHING SKILLS

Sister Lula Bell came back into the room with a surprised look on her face. She told them, "I cannot believe you all are still here. Doesn't everybody have their own houses to go to? Just in case you all do not know, my mother's house is not a hangout spot. You all do not have to go home, but you do have to leave here." Preacher-man Wannado was still at it. In his preacher voice, he said to her, "We know this house is not a hangout spot, but Mother Rongway is in the kitchen as we speak, and I know she is cooking a delicious meal. The Good Book says they that wait upon the food shall renew their strength. They can go jogging and not faint. They can go for a walk and not get hungry." Then he asked, "Can I get an *Amen*?" They all said, "Amen."

Sister Knowsall briefly forgot that she was upset with Minister Wannado and started smiling from ear-to-ear. She said with excitement in her voice, "That is another reason I just love that man, he knows how to quote them scriptures." Sister Aintwright said, "I must agree. Minister Wannado is truly gifted in the word. People say he is one of those word preachers." Sister Lula Bell, trying to egg him on, told minister Wannado, "Since you're all that and a bag of chips, give us a word." Deacon Aintwright got so excited he began to jump around like a child at Christmas with a new toy. He shouted and said, "That is what

I want to hear! We are getting ready to have some church up in here!" Minister Wannado began to moan as he got into his preacher mode.

He said, "Members of the Rongway First Liberation Church, I would like to tell everybody a story about a little old shepherd boy name David. Can I get an *Amen* up in here?" Just at that moment, Mother Rongway and Mother Runnamouth came in, and they both got excited. Mother Rongway shouted, "Oh, glory! I thought I heard Minister Wannado tuning up in here. Go head-on and preach, boy, preach! Let the Lord use you." Mother Runnamouth shouted and told him, "Go ahead. I want to get my shout on up in here, so give us a word." Minister Wannado began to preach. He began to say, "They tell me that Mary had a little lamb that used to follow her everywhere she went. But one day Mary got tired of that lamb following her around, so she hired that boy David to babysit her little lamb. Can I get an *Amen*? Can I get a *Thank you, Jesus*?"

Sister Knowsall was excited and began jumping around the room like a chicken. She screamed and told Minister Wannado, "Go on and say that word. You know you are preaching now. That is my boo." He continued in his preacher voice. He said, "They tell me, one day, little old David had to go fight a giant, because that boy loved to fight. So, he left that poor little lamb home alone. Can I get an *Amen*?" Sister Aintwright, in a high-pitched voice filled with excitement, shouted loudly and told Minister Wannado, "Come on, preacher man. I want to cut some flips up in here." Deacon Aintwright got excited and said, "I do too. Preach, Wannado, preach. Huff and puff and preach this house down. Let the Lord use you."

Minister Wannado resumed his sermon with his preacher moan. He said, "They tell me when David left that lamb home alone, Sister Red Robinhood and her big bad wolf stopped by, and they had lamb chops for dinner. And that was when the songwriter got the idea to write the song, 'Oh Mary Don't You Weep.' Can I get an *Amen*? Can I get a *Thank you, Jesus*? Can I get a *hallelujah*?" Sister Lula Bell, laughing, said, "I forgot how anointed Minister Wannado is. You can preach to me any day, or night too, for that matter." Mother Rongway started jumping up and down and screaming. She said, "That is my boy right there. He has more anointing in his big toe than Pastor Whocares has in his whole body. I do not know why I did not make him the pastor of the church. You never know; things might change around here." Mother Runnamouth, all excited, told Mother Rongway, "I do not see why you did not make Minister Wannado pastor in the first place. Everybody knows Pastor Whocares does not care about anybody but himself, and he sure cannot preach like that. I do not know anybody who can preach like this preacher boy can."

Sister Knowsall told Mother Runnamouth, "I know you are talking right. I like Pastor Whocares, and he is an all-right preacher, but he cannot hold a candle to my boo. He is just too gifted." Deacon Aintwright, with excitement in his voice, said, "I could have told you all that Minister Wannado is a bad man. Minister Wannado is so bad, I have even seen him walking on ice. I bet Minister Wannado can even part the Mississippi River." Sister Aintwright, excited like everybody else, told Cletus, "You have never lied. Minister Wannado is bad to the bone. He is on a whole different level than everybody else."

Minister Wannado was finishing his sermon, and said, "I am getting ready to close." He began to moan again and said, "But before I do, I want to ask you all a question. If you need somebody to watch your little lamb, who you gonna call?" They all shouted, "David!" He asked, "If you need somebody to kill your giant, who you gonna call?" They all shouted, "David!" He asked, "If you need somebody to make lamb chops and gravy, who you gonna call?" They all shouted, "Sister Red Robinhood!" Then he asked, "Can I get an *Amen*? Can I get a *Hallelujah*? Can I get a *Thank you, Jesus*? Can I get a glass of orange juice?" Sister Lula Bell shouted out and said, "You do not need any orange juice. Somebody needs to get the offering plate. Anybody that preaches as hard as Minister Wannado preaches needs to get paid. We need to take up a love offering, and I will give the first fifty cents myself."

Mother Rongway started laughing and told Lula Bell, "You are just like me: too generous. I believe you will give the clothes off your back if it will help somebody." Mother Runnamouth walked over to Minister Wannado and leaned in close to him. She whispered and told him, "Take my advice. Do not quit your day job. If everybody is as generous as those two, you and Sister Knowsall will starve to death." Sister Knowsall agreed and said to Minister Wannado, "By the way, just so you know, when we get married, I will not be working anymore, so I suggest you get another job other than preaching." Minister Wannado replied in his preacher voice. He told her, "Hold on my paper sack tan queen. The Good Book does say if a woman doesn't work, she doesn't eat." Deacon Aintwright stuck out his chest and agreed with Minister Wannado. He told him, "Tell her while I listen. I read that same scripture myself. Besides Bertha Mae knows the deal."

Sister Aintwright looked at him and got upset and loud. "The only reason I went to work in the first place was because Mother Rongway had you put in jail for stealing money from the church. I know you have only been out of jail for a week and have not had time to find another job yet, but just as soon as you get one, I am quitting my job. Do not go getting all high and mighty because you are the one who knows the deal." Now Deacon Aintwright got upset. He asked her, "Why do you want to bring that up again? Since I got out of jail, every chance you get, you throw it up in my face. I have had enough. I am tired of you embarrassing me everywhere we go, so you need to keep your mouth closed." Sister Aintwright looked surprised. She told him, "I know you are not trying to get all huffy with me just because you are in front of everybody. I will stomp you through this floor in Mother Rongway's house. If you are a criminal, just admit it. It is not my fault you got caught stealing again after Mother Rongway warned you and you had to go to jail."

Sister Lula Bell, smiling and frowning at the same time, told them to hold up. She said, "I did not hear anything about that. I want to know, when did all that happen?" She looked at Mother Rongway and said,

"You tell me everything else; why you did not tell me that? How could you keep something that juicy from me?" Mother Rongway replied in her soft, motherly voice and told Lula Bell, "You should know that I am not the one to spread gossip, but the real truth is, I forgot all about that." Sister Lula Bell told Mother Rongway, "You know you do not forget anything, so do not even try to play me like that." Mother Runnamouth, with a serious voice, told Lula Bell, "You are right about that. Your mother does not forget anything."

Then Lula Bell said, "Enough about my mother. Let us get back to Deacon and Sister Aintwright. That was just starting to get good. One of you guys needs to throw the first punch." Minister Wannado, in his preacher voice, once again tried to intervene. He told them, "'Vengeance is mine saith the Lord', but just in case He doesn't get here in time, go ahead and take matters into your own hands. Sister Lula Bell told them, "Minister Wannado is right, and since I am your friend, I will be glad to move the furniture so you guys will have plenty of room." Sister Knowsall jumped at the opportunity. She said to Sister Lula Bell, "Hold on, I will give you a hand moving the furniture. I have been waiting a long time to see Sister Aintwright kick Deacon Aintwright's back end." They began moving furniture around.

Then Mother Rongway became even louder. She told everybody to just calm down. She said, "There is not going to be any fighting up in my house unless I do it. I like all of you, but everybody needs to leave my house before I call the police and you all leave in a squad car in handcuffs." Minister Wannado shouted at Sister Knowsall and asked her, "How can you tell them to do that? You know Sister Aintwright will hurt Deacon Aintwright. Come on, we need to leave so we can get dressed for the wedding." Sister Knowsall said, "I forgot all about that." She told Deacon Aintwright, "I am sorry, and we will see you and Sister Aintwright a little bit later." They both left. Deacon Aintwright snarled at his wife and said to her, "We are leaving too. I told you a hundred times that your mouth was going to get us in trouble, but I am not going back to jail, not even for you."

She looked at him and said, "Whatever. I may talk a lot, but I am not the one with the criminal record, so you should not get it twisted. You are just one step away from going back to jail anyway, and I am not going to jail because of you either, so we better leave." They left. Mother Runnamouth sat down disappointed and upset. She said, "I thought we were about to see a good, old-fashioned beatdown. I have not seen one of those in a long time." Sister Lula Bell laughed and agreed. She said, "I wanted to see that myself. I would have loved seeing Sister Aintwright in action. From what I hear that sister is not a joke, but my mother had to go and spoil everything." Mother Rongway started laughing and told Lula Bell, "You better believe Sister Aintwright is not a joke. She would have beaten Deacon Aintwright like a cheap set of drums." They all laughed. Mother Runnamouth, still laughing, said, "Poor Deacon Aintwright is not anything but skin and bones. It looks like Sister Aintwright eats all the food and will not let the deacon get any." They all laughed again. Sister Lula Bell, still laughing, said, "I bet Sister Aintwright makes him do all the cooking too. I do not know if you two knew it or not, but Sister Aintwright is one lazy sister." They all laughed again.

Suddenly, Toddie came into the room upset, screaming that she wanted to know what was so funny. She asked them, "How can I get my beauty sleep with you three making so much noise? What is going on in here?" Mother Rongway, in her sweet, motherly voice, told her they were sorry. She said, "We did not mean to disturb you, but you know how loud Mother Runnamouth and your aunt Lula Bell can get." Mother Runnamouth got an attitude and told Mother Rongway, "If my memory serves me right, you were laughing just as hard as we were." Sister Lula Bell got an attitude and asked her mother, "How can you sit there and act like you are all innocent, like you weren't laughing too?" Toddie walked over to the couch, sat down, and told her grandmother that it was all right. She told her, "I know how people are always trying to blame you for stuff you did not do."

Mother Rongway started fake crying and told Toddie, "I thank God for you. I am so glad that somebody can finally see and understand what I go through all the time." Mother Runnamouth stood up and told them, "I am going back in the kitchen." She started walking toward the kitchen and said, "I know lightning is about to strike any minute, and I do not want to get struck." Sister Lula Bell agreed and said, "I think we all better get up out of here." She told Toddie, "You are on your own." She told Mother Runnamouth, "Hold up, I am right behind you." They both left. Toddie stood up, walked over to her grandmother, and put her arm around her. She yelled to Lula Bell and said, "You do not have to worry about us. I heard that lightning does not strike twice in the same place. Once it strikes grandmother, I should be all right." Mother Rongway looked at Toddie and said, "For a minute there I thought you had some sense, but evidently I was mistaken."

CHAPTER 14

Mother Rongway went too far

At that moment, the doorbell rang. She told Toddie, "Go see who that is at the door before you say something that is going to get your ole grandmother upset." Grumbling, Toddie asked, "Why do I have to keep going to the door? All day long I have been going to the door." She walked over to the door and screamed, asking who was there. A voice shouted from the other side of the door and said, "It is Pastor and First Lady Whocares. Can we come in?" Toddie, now upset, screamed loudly, "No, go away! There is nobody home!" Then she turned and walked out of the room. Mother Rongway began talking to herself and said, "That Toddie is going to make me lose my religion." Then she shouted, "Just a minute!" as she opened the door. She spoke and told Pastor and First Lady Whocares, "Come on in and make yourselves at home." Pastor Whocares spoke in his normal upbeat voice and said, "Praise the Lord, Mother Rongway." The first lady spoke and told Mother, "I have not seen you since the last time," as she and Mother pretended to hug one another. It was clear to see there was still some friction between these two. Mother Rongway asked, "What brings my pastor and the first lady by my house today? I know you two did not come over here to eat. It is not Sunday afternoon yet, so you folks are a little early." She started to laugh.

Pastor Whocares told her, "No, we did not come here to eat. I heard some news that upset me, and me and the first lady are here to talk to you about it." The first Lady agreed and told Mother Rongway, "We already know, since you are the mother of the church, that you are not one for starting any trouble." Mother told her, "You are so right. I will do all that I can to keep trouble from starting. I am a godly woman, and that is just the way I live, so the Lord can use me any way He sees fit." She raised both hands to the Lord in a hypocritical praise. Pastor Whocares, sounding a little upset, told her, "I have to be straight with you. What is all this talk I have been hearing about Missionary Scareaway getting married, and why was I not asked to do the ceremony? After all, I am the pastor of the church."

Mother Rongway replied very calmly and sweetly with a fake smile on her face. She told him, "Maybe it is a need-to-know-only situation, and maybe I did not feel you needed to know. May I remind you who owns the church and that you were hired to do whatever I tell you to do, and nothing else." At this point, First Lady Whocares raised both hands and shouted out with a loud voice, really upset. She cried out, "Lord Jesus; I stretch my hands to thee, because if I do not, I am going to punch this old demon in her wrinkled-up old face." Pastor Whocares, trying to remain calm himself, told his wife, "Calm down. Getting violent is not the answer. We came over here to talk with Mother Rongway, not to start a fight with her." Mother Rongway told the first lady, "You better listen to your husband, because he is an incredibly wise man, and he is concerned about your health. I would hate to put you in a coma."

The first lady, with tears in her eyes, asked her husband, "What is wrong with you? Are you going to stand there and let Mother Rongway disrespect me like that? If you do not put her in her place, I am leaving you and moving back home with my mother." Mother Rongway shouted "Hallelujah" and told the first lady, "I am so glad to hear you say that. Now I do not have to pretend that I like you anymore, because you get on my nerves." The first lady, now sobbing, once again asked Clyde, "What is wrong with you? Do you hear the way this crazy old woman is talking to me?" He told her, "You should just calm down. Maybe we came at a bad time. Maybe Mother Rongway is having a bad hair day, and I am sure she did not mean all that." Mother Rongway quickly spoke up and said, "Yes, I did. I did not stutter." She told the first lady, "Look at me and read my lips. I do not like you, never did like you, and never will like you."

Now the first lady was fuming. She screamed at her husband and told him, "I thought I married a man, but I now see I did not. I am leaving, because I do not have to stay here and take this abuse and watch my cowardly husband bow down to this demon." Pastor Whocares spoke with authority and said to the first lady, "Hold up. I will handle it." He told Mother Rongway, "I like you, but I think you went a little too far this time. If you will apologize to Shirley, I am sure everything will be forgotten and forgiven." Mother Rongway laughed and told him, "You must be joking. Why should I apologize for telling the truth? The Good Book does say, and I think it is Third or Fourth Corinthians, to tell the truth and stay in the church. That is precisely what I have done."

First Lady Whocares continued to cry hard. She told Clyde, "That is it. If you want to stay here in this broke-down old town and pastor that demonic church, you can go right ahead. I am leaving." Mother Rongway looked at her and said, "Poor first lady. I feel so bad for you, and I know precisely what I should do. To show you that there are no hard feelings and that I forgive you, I will help you pack." Pastor Whocares asked Mother, "Can me and Shirley have a few minutes alone? We need to have a little talk." Mother Rongway replied in her sweet, motherly voice and told him of course. She said, "I will do anything for my pastor. I will be in the other room if you need me." She went out of the room. The first lady was still upset and told Clyde, "We need to leave. We do not have anything to talk about unless it is how fast we can get out of this town."

Pastor Whocares began to plead with her. He asked her, "Have you forgotten about that fat paycheck I get every week? Not to mention all the other perks we get, furs, new cars, and free rent." The first lady could not believe what she was hearing. She told him, "I do not care what that ungodly woman gave you to keep you her stoolie. Mother Rongway can be giving you a million dollars a week; I do not care. I cannot take any more of Mother's abuse." Pastor Whocares, still pleading with her, asked her, "Where else am I going to find another job paying me this kind of money? Remember, if we give this up, you will have to get a job. Is that what you want to do?" She looked him straight in his eyes and said, "At this point, I do not care if I have to pick up cans alongside the road. I am getting out of that so-called church. I have had it up to my nose, and it is starting to smell pretty bad in here."

Pastor Whocares kept pleading with First Lady Whocares. He begged her to calm down. He told her, "Mother Rongway is just getting old, and you need to learn to ignore her. That is what I do all the time." The first lady asked him, "Have you lost your mind, or are you just plain stupid. If you cannot see that Mother Rongway is the devil's spawn, you need some serious help." Pastor Whocares got stern and told Shirley, "That is enough. I am going to call Mother back in here so we can apologize to her and do whatever it takes. I am not giving up that money." The first lady asked him, "Have you become so money-hungry that you are willing to stoop that low?" Sympathetically, she asked him, "What happened to you? You have been a different person since we came to this town and that church." He told her, "I do not know what you are talking about, because there is not anything wrong with me. Is there something wrong with me wanting to get paid?" She told him, "Yes, there is something wrong with it if it means you have to sell your soul to the devil. The way I see it, you sold your soul to Mother Rongway, and cheaply if you ask me." He said to her, "You should know that isn't true." He reminded her of what he told her before: "I am my own man, and nobody can tell Pastor Whocares what to do." She said to him, "All right, then. Since you are so bad, prove it. Call Mother Rongway back in here and put her in her place, and I will believe you."

Pastor Whocares finally found his backbone. He told his wife he would. He stuck out his chest and shouted to Mother Rongway. He asked her, "Will you come back in the room, please?" Mother Rongway came into the room in her usual arrogant manner. In her sweet, motherly voice, she said to Pastor Whocares, "I hope you had enough time to set the first lady straight. It was clear to see she was confused." Pastor Whocares, with a firm voice, said, "No, I did not. In fact, the first lady straightened me out, and I think you owe both of us an apology." Mother Rongway was shocked. She told him, "Wait a minute. My ears must be playing tricks on me, because I think I heard you say I owe the two of you an apology." First Lady Whocares, gloating, spoke up and told Mother Rongway, "That is most definitely what you heard. Pastor Whocares did not stutter, and we are not leaving here until you apologize." At that moment Mother began laughing uncontrollably and called out to her daughter Lula Bell. She told her, "You better fix up the spare bedroom, because the pastor and the first lady are moving in." Pastor Whocares interrupted Mother and told her, "That will not be necessary. You just need to apologize, that is all. I am the pastor, and you need to stay in your place and let me run the church the way I think it should be run."

First Lady Whocares felt proud and said, "That is the man I married. I knew you had a backbone in there somewhere." But Mother Rongway always came out on top. She put her hands on her hips and moved her head from side to side. She told them, "You two have twenty-four hours to pack up and get out of the house you are living in rent-free, which belongs to me, and get out of my church." She told the pastor, "You are fired." After hearing that, Pastor Whocares fell on his knees and began to beg. He told Mother Rongway, "I was wrong, and I apologize. I do not care; you can run the church and I will do whatever you tell me to do. Just do not fire me. I beg you, please!" Mother, holding up her hand, told him, "It is too late, and you can talk to the hand. I suggest the two of you get to stepping." The first lady looked at Clyde in disgust and upset and told him, "We should go before you make a complete idiot out of yourself, but you have already done that. I have never been so embarrassed in all my life. Get up off your knees like a puppy and let's go." They left.

Mother Rongway yelled and called Toddie and asked her, "Will you come in here where I am? I need you to do something for me." At that moment, Toddie rushed in, thinking something was wrong. She asked her grandmother, "Is everything all right? You sound like you are upset about something." Mother Rongway told her, "I just need you to go to the store and get me something for my headache. Those church folk are trying to drive me out of my mind." Toddie told her, "Sure, no problem. You just sit there and relax, and I will be right back." She left. Once again Mother Rongway yelled and called Lula Bell and Mother Runnamouth. She asked them, "Will the both of you come in here for a minute?" They both came in. Sister Lula Bell was concerned and asked her mother, "What is going on? You look upset. Is everything all right?" Mother Runnamouth also asked Mother Rongway, "What is wrong? You know you cannot fool me, because I know you too well for that."

Mother Rongway told them, "Everything is not all right. I just had to fire Pastor Whocares, and I am a little upset." Sister Lula Bell was shocked and told Mother Rongway, "Stop playing. And what do you mean you fired Pastor Whocares? How could you fire the pastor?" Mother Rongway told her, "He went too far this time. He had the nerve to try and put me in my place. I believe for a minute he forgot who I am and who runs the church." Mother Runnamouth, with a confused look on her face, said to Mother Rongway, "I thought the pastor was the one who ran the church." Mother Rongway told her, "Now you know. Nobody runs my church but me. I am going to my room to take a nap because my head is pounding." She got up and left the room.

Mother Runnamouth looked at Sister Lula Bell, still confused. She told Sister Lula Bell, "I do not mean any harm, but I think your mother has lost it. Who ever heard of the mother of the church firing the pastor? I have heard some crazy stuff before, but I have never heard anything like this." Sister Lula Bell reluctantly looked at Mother Runnamouth and said, "Normally I would try to defend my mother, but this time I too think she went too far. My mother is on her own with this one." Mother Runnamouth told her, "I have known your mother for many years, and to be honest, I have seen her do some dirty stuff, and I did not say a word, but I cannot go along with her on this one." A few minutes passed and Mother Rongway came back into the room, still upset, and yelled as she sat down. She said, "The nerve of that woman." Sister Lula Bell asked her, "What is wrong with you now? I thought you were going to take a nap, and what woman are you talking about?" Mother Rongway told her, "I just got off the phone with Evangelist Scareaway, and she called herself putting me in my place."

Mother Rongway was terribly upset. Mother Runnamouth, now upset herself, told Mother Rongway, "I know you got her straight. How does she think she can put somebody in their place when she needs to be put in her place?" Sister Lula Bell started laughing and asked them, "Are you two talking about Evangelist Gertrude Scareaway, Missionary Scareaway's aunt? That woman is a trip." Mother Rongway agreed and said, "I am too through with her. That woman must not know who she is messing with, but she is about to find out." Mother Runnamouth asked her, "Did you at least get a chance to tell her off?" Lula Bell told her, "Knowing my mother, she went up one side of Evangelist Scareaway and down the other. I bet right now that poor woman is somewhere in a corner licking her wounds." They both laughed. Mother Rongway, smiling and shaking her head, told them, "No, I did not at the time, but I have her number. Where is the telephone? I need to make a call."

Mother Runnamouth told her, "That is more like it. If anybody can put Evangelist Scareaway in her place, I know Mother Rongway can." Sister Lula Bell said, "I know that is right. I have seen my mother go toe-to-toe with the best of them, and when the smoke cleared, she was the only one left standing." Suddenly, Mother Rongway picked up the telephone and began to dial. She told them, "I am not calling Evangelist Scareaway." She paused, then said, "Hello, Brother Moanback, this is Mother Rongway." She paused. She told him, "I am doing fine. How are you doing?" She paused. "That is good, and I am glad to hear it. The reason I am calling you is because Missionary Scareaway asked me to give you a call because she is too upset to call you herself." She paused. He must have asked if there was something wrong, because she told him, "Yes, I guess you can say something is wrong. Missionary Scareaway wants me to let you know that the wedding is off." She paused. She told him, "I do not know why, and the missionary did not give me a reason; she just said it is over between the two of you." She paused. She then told him, "I do not blame you, because if it were me, I would be leaving on the first thing smoking too." She paused. She told him, "The missionary said you should not try to call her because she does not want to talk to you." She paused and then told him, "Okay, and I will keep you in my prayers," and she said goodbye. She hung up the phone.

Mother Runnamouth was in shock. She screamed and asked Mother Rongway, "What did you just do? Missionary Scareaway is going to be devastated." Sister Lula Bell, also in shock, told her Mother, "I know you can be cruel, but I did not know how cruel until just now. I do not think I like you very much anymore." Mother Rongway felt no remorse. She told them, "That so-called Evangelist Scareaway went too far this time. She should not have crossed me, because now everybody is going to pay." Mother Runnamouth told her, "I believe this time you went too far. I really thought Missionary Scareaway was one of your girls. How could you do that to your girl, and what are you going to tell her?" Sister Lula Bell told Mother Runnamouth, "You do not have to worry about that. Knowing my mother as I do, I am sure she will come up with a lie that will peel paint off bricks."

Mother Rongway said, "I will just tell her what he told me on the telephone. He said he was leaving town and never coming back this way again." Sister Lula Bell said, "What else could he say after what you told him? And he is not the only one leaving town. In fact, I think I will move to another state." She then told Mother Rongway, "Do me a favor and do not tell anybody that I am your daughter." She left the room. Mother Rongway got upset and loudly told her, "Go on and leave! I do not need you anyway. I am Mother Rongway, and everybody knows who I am." Mother Runnamouth looked at her and told her, "I do not doubt that at all, and if they do not already know who you are, they will after this." She then told Mother Rongway, "I do not want to know you anymore. I am going to find me another church to go to, no matter how far I have to drive." She told Mother Rongway goodbye and stood up to leave.

Mother Rongway, trembling as she stood up, asked Mother Runnamouth, "What are you talking about? You and I have been friends for more than twenty years. How can you throw our friendship away that easily?" She told Mother Rongway, "You have a problem, and you need help. Until you realize that, I do not want to be your friend anymore. I do not even want to be around you anymore." She headed for the door. At this point, Mother Rongway walked behind Mother Runnamouth and began yelling again, telling her, "Go on and leave. I do not need you either. I have a lot of friends." She got up but immediately sat back down, crying and asking the Lord, "What have I done? My best friend is gone. This is all that so-called Evangelist Scareaway's fault!"

Once more, the doorbell rang. She jumped up, excited, and ran to the door. She thought it was Mother Runnamouth coming back. She yelled and said, "I knew you would come back." She opened the door and was instantly disappointed. It was just some more church people. She told them to come in and went and sat back down. Deacon and Sister Aintwright and Elder and Sister Backnibbler came in, and Deacon Aintwright began to talk, and he was terribly upset. He asked Mother Rongway, "Is it true what I heard about you firing Pastor Whocares and canceling Missionary Scareaway's wedding? Please tell me that is not true." Sister Aintwright was also upset and told Mother Rongway, "Your daughter, Lula Bell, called us and told us what you have done. How could you do something that low-down and dirty? Sister Backnibbler, upset and angry, told Mother, "I have heard of people doing some nasty, low-down stuff before, but that is the lowest. You should be in the *Guinness Book of World Records* because you just set a world record for being the most devious person who ever lived."

Elder Backnibbler, shaking his head said, "I never thought the mother of the church would do something like that. You are one heartless old woman. Me and sister Backnibbler have decided we do not want to be members of your church anymore. We should never have come back when we left the first time." He said goodbye, and they left. Deacon Aintwright told Mother Rongway, "Me and Bertha Mae decided to do the same thing. We should have left when I got out of jail, but Bertha Mae did not want to leave. I must say, what you did this time is the last straw. We are leaving." He told his wife to come along and they left together.

Mother Rongway broke down again and started crying uncontrollably. She began talking to herself again and asked, "Why is this happening to me? I only did what I thought was best. I do not see why everybody else could not see that." Just then the doorbell rang again. She said to herself, "Now what?" She got up and opened the door. It was Evangelist Trying and Deaconess Donothing. She told them to come on in. She went back and sat down, waiting to hear more bad news. Evangelist Trying, doing all she could to hold back the tears in her eyes, asked Mother Rongway, "What is going on? I heard that you fired the Pastor and have canceled Missionary Scareaway's wedding. Me and Missionary Scareaway did not always get along, but I would not wish that on anybody. I cannot even imagine what the missionary is going through right now." Deaconess Donothing looked at Mother Rongway and said, "I know what she might be feeling. If it were me, I would probably be wishing I were dead. She told Mother Rongway, "You are one evil woman, and you are going straight to hell."

Mother Rongway, still crying, said, "I made a little mistake. So what? People make mistakes all the time, and I am only human. Where is everybody's compassion?" Evangelist Trying looked at her and told her, "What you did was not a mistake; that was malicious and devastating. I am sure you have destroyed poor Missionary Scareaway. I do not want to be a member of your church anymore. I do not want to have anything else to do with you." She told the deaconess they needed to go. Deaconess Donothing agreed and told Mother Rongway, "After what you have done, I do not want to know that I knew you. I am leaving your church too, and you can keep that money you owe me." They both left.

Mother got an attitude and got loud and yelled at them and said, "Fine, leave! Everybody else is leaving, so why should you two be any different?" Then she asked, "Don't I at least deserve a second chance?" She sat there crying, all alone. Poor Mother Rongway. A little while later the doorbell rang again. Mother said to herself, "Here we go again," and went to the door. It was Minister Wannado and Sister Knowsall. Mother told them, "Come on in. You all please excuse the way I look, but I am having a bad hair day." She sat back down. Minister Wannado spoke in his usual preacher voice and said, "The Lord is still good, and He is still blessing me right now. I heard some disturbing news, and it hurts me to my heart to know that you could do something like that. Please say it is not so." Sister Knowsall, with pain in her voice, asked Mother Rongway, "How could you do that? Poor Missionary Scareaway. I know she has to be going out of her mind. I do not think you realize what you have done."

Mother Rongway tried to plead her case. She said to Minister Wannado, "Out of all the members of my church, you should understand. You know you are my favorite preacher, and I am about to make you pastor of the church." Minister Wannado told Mother Rongway, "Well now, that changes things!" He was ready to jump at the opportunity, but Sister Knowsall snapped him out of it. She shouted at him in disbelief and asked him, "Have you lost your mind? You better not even think about it." Minister Wannado reluctantly told her she was right and told Mother, "No thank you. I cannot pastor your church, not with you telling me what to do. Me and Sister Knowsall have decided it will be best to leave your church before you do something to mess up our wedding. Besides that, I do not want to go to jail again . . ." He paused, looked around, and finished, "For shooting an old woman."

Sister Knowsall told Mother, "He is right; we are leaving your church. We should have left when you first started blackmailing me, but I wanted to believe you would change. Looking at you now and knowing what you have done, I see that will never happen. You are worse than I could have imagined." They said goodbye to Mother Rongway and left. Now in total chaos, Mother Rongway was truly upset. She said, "Everything that I have worked so hard for is falling apart. What am I going to do?" Once again, the doorbell rang. She said to herself, "I cannot take any more of this." She got up and opened the door. It was Missionary Scareaway, Evangelist Scareaway, and Brother June Bug stopping by one last time. Mother Rongway said to them, "I guess you all came over here to finish me off." She told them to come on in. She sat back down. Missionary Scareaway, with a weak voice and bloodshot eyes from crying so much, asked Mother, "How could you do that to me? Firing Pastor Whocares was bad enough, but I have been one of your girls for years and done everything you ever asked me to do and never questioned you. So, I am asking you again, how could you do that to me?"

Mother Rongway, who was now crying harder, told Missionary Scareaway, "I am so sorry, and I did not mean to hurt you, but this was all your aunt's fault." Evangelist Scareaway, of course upset, shouted, "What do you mean this was my fault? The devil is a liar. This was all Rosalee Rongway's doing. I was not the one who called off my niece's wedding. That was you and you alone, and it was low-down and dirty." Brother June Bug, with tears in his eyes, told Mother Rongway, "You have finally done it this time. I did not think that even you, being as low-down and dirty as you are, could do something like that." Mother tried to defend herself. Screaming loudly and angrily, she told them, "Wait a minute, because I said it was not my fault." She told Brother June Bug, "Your heathen mother called me a lying demon, and everybody knows that is not true. I always tells it like I see it. It is not my fault if people misunderstand what I say, so do not blame me."

Missionary Scareaway, still crying, said to Mother, "There is no way to misunderstand what you did. It is evident to everyone that the only one you care about is yourself. You never gave it a second thought as to what your 'so-called' revenge might do to innocent people." Missionary Scareaway broke down again. Brother June Bug embraced Missionary Scareaway and told her, "I know you are hurting, but I promise you I will find Brother Moanback. You will still have your wedding, in spite of what that crazy woman did." Missionary Scareaway told Mother, "I am leaving your church, and I never want to see you again." They all headed for the door. Mother Rongway stood up and started begging. She begged Missionary Scareaway not to leave. She said to her, "Please give me a chance to explain." The missionary turned around and yelled at Mother, "There is nothing to explain; I am through with you." They all left, and Mother Rongway sat back down crying.

Just then, her granddaughter, Toddie, returned home from the store and came into the room. She shouted and asked her grandmother what was wrong. "Who bothered you and got you so upset like this? Just tell me, and I will put their lights out." Mother Rongway, still sobbing, told Toddie, "I messed up. Everybody has left my church, and I have no more members. Nobody even likes me anymore, so what am I going to do?" Toddie told her, "You need to snap out of it, and what do you mean you do not know what to do? You are Mother Rongway, and you do not need those people." Mother Rongway asked her, "What about my church? I do not have any members at my church anymore, and I will have to close the doors. I do not even have a pastor because I fired Pastor Whocares." Toddie told her, "Do not worry about those hypocrites. You are better off without them anyway. Just like you got them, you and me together can get some new members."

Just like that, Mother Rongway snapped back to her old self. She told Toddie, "You are absolutely right, because I am Mother Rongway. We are going to start over again, just the two of us. I will get me some new members and a new pastor. The Rongway First Liberation Church will be bigger and better than it was before." She stood up and told Toddie, "Come with me into the kitchen so we can get something to eat. I am hungry." Toddie smiled and told her, "That is the Rosalee Rongway I know. We Rongways always bounce back." They put their arms around each other's shoulders and headed for the kitchen. As they walked, they began to talk and try to come up with some ideas to get new members in the church. When they reached the kitchen, Mother Rongway began to fix them a snack while Toddie sat at the kitchen table.

Mother told Toddie, "The first thing we must do is find a pastor as greedy as Pastor Whocares was. If we can find somebody who loves money like he did, I know I can control him." Then she said, "Maybe with every new membership, I can offer them their own personal parking space at no charge." Toddie disagreed and said to Mother Rongway, "No, that is not a good idea; remember, you give me that money. If you stop charging for parking, I will have to get a job, and that is not happening." Toddie said, "I have an idea. You should offer happy hour after every service with free booze to everyone who joins the church. I know people will come from all over the state for that." Mother thought about it for a moment and said, "No, I do not think that is a good idea. If I do that, I will have a bunch of drunks in the church and I will not be able to control them, and I need people I can control."

Toddie agreed and said, "Yeah, it will not be easy to control drunk folk." Then Mother Rongway said, "Maybe I can put in a smoking section for those who smoke and put ashtrays on every seat in that section. I know that will attract a lot of people." Toddie told Mother Rongway, "That is fine if you think that will work, but do not ask me to clean that section. I know there will be cigarette and cigar butts all over the floor." Mother agreed and said, "You may be right about that, and that may not be a good idea either." Mother said, "I know what I can do. I will get rid of the no-children rule, and that will surely bring people in." Toddie looked at Mother Rongway and shook her head. She said, "I do not think that is a good idea. Children make a lot of noise, and I like to take a nap while service is going on." Mother Rongway said, "I do too. That is the best time to take a nap, and you are right, children will make too much noise for us to sleep." She finished fixing their snack and sat down with Toddie. She told Toddie, "We are going to have to come up with something to get new members, but for now let us sit here and eat and enjoy one another's company. You know that together we are unstoppable. The Rongways always bounce back, and this is not the end but just the beginning." Toddie agreed and they high fived each other, and we know they will be back.

The end, for now.

Dedication Page

This book is dedicated to my children, Kia, Michael, and Jameika. To my late mother, Mary Evans and my brother, Lee Curtis Evans. To all my grandchildren. To Pastor and Elder Zeigler and the saints of GFOC. To Pastor and First Lady Belcher and the saints of the Anointed Tabernacle. To the whole body of Christ. I hope this book put a smile on your face in a time when it may be difficult to smile.

Introduction

This is a fictional book about the mother of the church who also runs it. She owns the church. She hires a Pastor that loves money so she can tell him what he can and cannot do in her church. She lies to and manipulates everybody that she come in contact with. She is a master at what she does and no one has ever been able to outwit her. Follow along as she causes all kind of chaos among the church members to the point they all walk out.

Printed in the USA
CPSIA information can be obtained
at www.ICGtesting.com
CBHW060342070824
12784CB00054B/729